All I V
Co ...y

All I Wanted Was Company

JOHN HOPKINS

ARCADIA BOOKS
LONDON

Arcadia Books Ltd
15–16 Nassau Street
London WIN 7RE

First published in Great Britain 1999
© John Hopkins 1999

A catalogue record for this book is available
from the British Library.

ISBN 1–900850–23–0

Typeset in Monotype Fournier by Discript, London WC2N 4BL
Printed in the United Kingdom by Biddles Ltd, Guildford

Arcadia Books distributors are as follows:
in the UK and elsewhere in Europe:
Turnaround Publishers Services
Unit 3, Olympia Trading Estate
Coburg Road
London N22 6TZ

in the USA and Canada:
Consortium Book Sales and Distribution, Inc.
1045 Westgate Drive
St Paul, MN 55114–1065

in Australia:
Tower Books
PO Box 213
Brookvale, NSW 2100

in New Zealand:
Addenda
Box 78224
Grey Lynn
Auckland

in South Africa:
Peter Hyde Associates (Pty) Ltd
PO Box 2856
Cape Town 8000

For E. A. and the boys

ALICE AND I came to Tangier about a year ago. We had been doing some travelling and had wound up in Paris. I don't like Paris much, or any big city for that matter. Although I am practically a New Yorker myself, city life has always seemed to me to require too much effort. The pace of life is too fast and unnatural, and I am quite unable to keep up with it. I tire easily, so I usually end up sitting around doing nothing.

I was doing just that – having a beer in one of those French cafés and telling a fellow at the next table how much I disliked Paris. The traffic was thundering by and, although we sat only three feet apart, we practically had to shout to make ourselves understood. He suggested that, since Paris disagreed with me, I ought to go down to Tangier and see how I liked it there. Morocco is more like the way the world used to be, he said – cleaner and quieter. He was a swarthy fellow with a shining smile; that's where he came from himself.

The idea appealed to me. I'd heard some other good things about Morocco, such as you can live there without spending too much money, the sun shines all the time, and the beaches rank among the best in the world. I went back to the hotel to ask Alice what she thought about it. She was still in bed, smoking cigarettes and reading magazines. It was a bad hour for her. We had been up late the night before. But her face retains just enough hardness not to fall out of shape. Alice is solid, but not pudgy.

'Norman,' she said, 'where have you been?'

I told her I'd been sitting in a café talking to a fellow about Morocco. That seemed to interest her. I explained my desire to get out of Paris and raised the possibility of going to some sunny place like Tangier. She thought about it for a minute before telling me to go down to the airline ticket office to check on plane schedules. I did, and found there was a flight the next day. I took out my travellers cheques and bought two tickets on the spot. When I got back to the hotel and showed them to Alice, she laughed and said I'd better start packing right away, knowing how long it took me to get my things together.

The next day we landed in Tangier, and it wasn't long before we realized we were going to like it. We took a room in an attractive hotel with a view of the sea. Alice called up some English people she knew who lived there, and they started inviting us to cocktail parties. The weather was warm, and I went to the beach nearly every day. Although I have never learned how to swim properly, I am not afraid to wade out up to my shoulders when the water is calm, which it almost always is during summer in the Bay of Tangier, when the east wind isn't blowing. Alice, of course, started looking around for things to export to her shop in New York. Now I know why she was interested in coming to Morocco in the first place. Indigenous crafts are her hobby and business.

*

I met Alice the day I walked into her shop to sell some *huacos* or Inca pots I had brought back from Peru. She took them and asked if I had any more. I did: in Peru I had gone on an archaeological dig in a desert valley where it hadn't rained in a hundred years. Grave robbers had already visited that place where time seemed to have stopped. Gold was what they had been after; but scattered on the sand among the skulls and bones from the looted tomb were delicate examples of cloth and pottery whose dry, dusty smell conveyed the mystery of a vanished civilization – just there for the picking.

Soon Alice and I were in business together. I think she took a liking to me from the beginning. We saw more and more of each other. She enjoyed racing around New York with me on the back of my motorcycle. Some people raised their eyebrows, but Alice didn't care and neither did I. One day she asked me if I would like to do some more travelling. We had often talked of visiting other countries. I had wandered around South America a bit, and my stories used to amuse her.

Of course I said yes.

'Well,' she said, 'keep yourself free.'

A few weeks later she announced that she was going to turn the shop over to a friend. She wanted to get out of New York and see some of the world 'before it was too late,' and asked if I wanted to come along. Naturally, I was all for it.

We went straight to the bank, where she bought a pile of travellers cheques.

'Half for you, half for me,' she said, pushing a bunch my way for me to sign.

'You're giving me all these travellers cheques?' I asked. 'Why?'

'What if I drop dead in some foreign city? You'll need money to get home on.'

'Take it back,' I said.

'All right. I'm sorry I said it.'

'Take it back again!'

'OK! I was just kidding.'

'Jokes like that make me nervous.'

Soon we were on our way to Europe. At our going away party a fellow made a crack about gigolos. I didn't mind, but Alice happened to over-hear. She came over and let him have it full blast. That's what I like about Alice — she never holds anything back. While I was searching for the right words to defend myself, she went on the offensive and started firing point-blank. She doesn't fool around, and her quickness and honesty never fail to clear the air. By the time she finished, that fellow wished he'd never opened his mouth.

Some people do think it odd for a young man and an older woman to travel together, but I don't agree. Alice has never told me her age. Her passport says she was born about the same year as my mother, but I don't see that that makes any difference. She has always been kind to me, and that is what matters.

✳

One day after lunch we got into a taxi and drove out to the Old Mountain, one of Tangier's residential districts. Alice wanted to have a look at a house up there. It was a simple enough place, whitewashed inside and out, but, when we walked onto the terrace, we were presented with a 180° panorama of the Strait of Gibraltar. The mountains of southern Spain floated like a dream across the water. Great ships slid from one ocean to another toward unknown destinations. The view gave the house a spiritual focus; it took the property into a different dimension. Can this be ours? I asked myself. Can we live here? The upper branches of the mimosa trees had been conveniently pruned so as not to obstruct the horizon.

On a side patio I spotted a pair of olive trees where I could sling my hammock. A parrot hanging upside down in a cage fixed us with a reptilian gaze.

At the top of some stairs we were shown a tower room which I correctly guessed would be mine. Cool, white and unadorned, it was furnished with a single bed, wooden table and chair. The more comfortable quarters where Alice would sleep were located downstairs – a large bedroom with french doors leading onto the terrace, full bath and closets – while I would have to make do with a basic shower stall.

While Alice went around with the real estate agent, I explored the garden. It was more of a wood than a garden, with little paths winding among the trees, and a pond where golden fish swam dreamily beneath the lily pads. The paths had been laid out in such a way that one couldn't be seen from another, which made you think you were taking the only path through the wood, when in fact there were many. I thought that was pretty smart.

We decided to take it. The rent was low, and Alice wasn't one to pass up a bargain. A few days later we moved in. Life began to take on order and meaning. We were able to unpack our suitcases for a change. I hung up my clothes, stood my books on the shelf next to the bed, and laid out my notebooks on the table.

Alice went over to Gibraltar and bought a car, not a proper car but one of those little German cars, which allowed us to go everywhere. Although I do have a driver's licence, I have never owned a car. Besides, I prefer motorcycles.

Alice says she can't drive either. Probably she forgot the time she told me she drove a truck while she was in the army. Therefore we hired a chauffeur to drive us about. At first I thought it was pretty silly to have a chauffeur for such a small car, but I soon got used to it and began to appreciate the luxury. The chauffeur also does some gardening around the house. His name is Mohamed.

*

The time passes quickly and easily in Tangier. The days all seem to be sunny and warm, but there isn't much to do except to go to the beach during the day and to bars at night. Alice keeps herself busy investigating the local arts and crafts. She and Mohamed drive around the countryside regularly, visiting the rural markets, buying up indigenous products, and shipping them off to America.

Consequently, I am left by myself much of the time, which I don't mind, for I like to nap in my hammock or read. It's like being cradled in air. Or I lie back with my hands behind my head, gaze up through the olive branches, and let my thoughts wander, occasionally jotting one of them down in a notebook.

I made some repairs and improvements around the house. I'm good at fixing things if they aren't too complicated. My father used to say I was good with my hands. Carpentry I enjoy the most; the plumbing I leave alone.

I painted the porch furniture the same turquoise-blue colour as the doors and shutters on the house. Part of the front wall holding the patio was falling down. I pulled it apart, mixed up cement and relaid the bricks, and covered it over with a layer of plaster.

For exercise I take my shoes off, so my feet will get tough, and walk down to the bottom of the Old Mountain, where the swimming is good. If the tide is out I wade in the rock pools, peering at the creatures who make their homes there. Afterwards I may order a glass of mint tea in one of the cafés the Moroccans build in summer from palm fronds and cane, and watch the fishermen cast their lines into the sea. It's a peaceful hour, especially toward the end of the day. I feel quite at home among the fishermen and their friends making quiet conversation while the waves lap the shore.

However, when Alice is away, I become uneasy at night. I usually stay up late reading until I can't keep my eyes open any longer. Fatima our maid has a room behind the kitchen. When sleep won't come, she makes mint tea and we sit up and converse in Spanish. She's even teaching me some words in Arabic. But mainly we talk about her family. She's worried that her *sobrina* won't get married, because she has a serious skin disease. Moreover, the girl is overweight, and her job at the telephone company doesn't pay much. Arranged marriages are the norm in Muslim society, but the girl's poor complexion and weight problem were making it difficult to find a suitable young man.

After a while I got restless and decided to go out looking for work. Any job is hard to find in Tangier, I soon discovered, and well-paid ones are practically non-existent. Furthermore, the Moroccans don't want foreigners coming in and snapping them up, which I could understand. I was welcome as a visitor, I was told, but not as a worker. If I wanted a job, then I needed a work permit, and they're hard to get. After a few days I gave up. I don't need the cash, of course, because Alice pays for everything. Every now and then I cash a travellers check for pocket money. So there is no rush. Something may turn up yet.

※

One time I accompanied Alice on a trip to the south of Morocco. We visited Fez and Marrakesh, cities I had heard so much about. I have to admit that I wasn't very happy in those places. The children never leave you alone, and finding your way through the maze of winding alleys is an unnerving experience for anyone used to the Manhattan grid.

At my request we made a trip over the Atlas Mountains to see the desert. I've always been curious about arid lands, because the air is pollen-free and easy to breathe. We made an early start. Mohamed had never driven in the mountains before. He scared us half to death racing around one hairpin turn after another where little shrines mark the places where some truck or bus had gone screaming into space. I was glad to leave the mountains behind. The sky grew bigger as the land levelled out. Ahead lay endless horizontal space with plateaux and ridges jutting and jutting until they fade into the haze of heat and distance. No wonder the ancients thought the earth was flat. And all the time the terrain became drier, until there was nothing but rock and sand. Mainly rock.

We arrived in a town called Zagora and checked into the tourist hotel in time for lunch. While Alice took a nap, I climbed the trail that winds around Zagora Mountain, in order to view the desert at sunset. The summit was littered with the ruins of an ancient fortress. Some say it was Arab; others that it was Portuguese and the word Zagora was the name of the daughter of the Portuguese commander, many years ago.

The sun was going down and the wind began to

blow. I could see for miles. I found the desert withering in its impersonality. The vast stony silence made me think of the judgement of God. It also made me realize that the Sahara cannot be a home for any outsider, except for one who passionately wishes it to be so.

A boy dressed in army fatigues jumped from behind a rock, startling me. I tried to talk to him but he only grunted. It dawned on me that he was a deaf mute. All of a sudden he began to perform cartwheels in an aggressive but very professional manner. He was quite an acrobat – an ugly one. Never had I seen such violent cartwheels. When his bare feet thudded down hard on the sunbaked earth, they kicked up explosions of dust, which the rising wind whisked away. His thick feet and splayed out toes looked as if they belonged to an animal. Abruptly, he ceased his spinning and held out his hand. I was glad he stopped; his cartwheels were beginning to make me dizzy. I gave him a coin. Without so much as a grunt of thanks, he leapt over the cliff and disappeared. I went to the edge and looked down. There he was, already far below, bounding down the mountainside that looked almost vertical. He was running in a cloud of dust and falling rock. The sun, meanwhile, had dropped below the horizon. The world, which a minute before had been filled with golden light, was suddenly plunged into a purple iridescence. So this is the desert, I thought, full of mysteries. I inhaled the dry air and experienced a profound sense of physical well-being.

Outside Zagora we came upon a hand-painted sign that showed men on camels riding off into the desert. TIMBUKTOO – 52 DAYS, the sign said. While Alice snapped photos, I mounted a camel reserved for tourists.

'Hey, Alice,' I shouted, 'how about you and me putting on some robes and riding down to Timbuktoo?'

'You can do that when I'm in the grave, wild man.'

'Hey, don't talk like that! Take it back!'

'All right. I was only kidding!'

'Take it back again!'

It was just an idea inspired by a romantic and colourful sign. I hadn't been on the camel more than a minute before I began to sneeze. The camel was another item to add to my list of allergies.

I was glad to return to Tangier. After a while the city gets a hold on one, and I have become reluctant to leave for any reason. We took other excursions to Chauen and Asilah, quaint Moroccan villages only an hour or so away. But despite the picturesque mountain landscape, or the old Portuguese ramparts pushing out into the sea, those places did not interest me. No sooner had we arrived than I wished we were back in Tangier. What with Mohamed to drive the car and Fatima to cook, I feel quite comfortable and content in our little house on the Mountain. As the days go by I grow less eager to interrupt the pleasant routine.

✳

Only one thing bothers me – my health. I have asthma pretty badly, as I have had since I was two years old. At first Tangier's climate seemed a healthy one, with warm and sunny days most of the year round, but the weather can be deceptively damp. Dampness has always caused me to suffer.

When I was a little boy growing up in New Jersey, my parents thought seriously about sending me to Arizona, where the climate is considered to be ideal for someone with asthma.

'Son,' my father asked, 'how would you like to go to school out west where you'll feel so much better?'

I was surprised when he said that. It was hard to understand why my father wanted to send me so far away from home.

When I replied, 'Yes, Dad, that will be fine. Maybe I'll become a cowboy out there, or start up a ranch,' he looked surprised. I believe I was expected to put up some resistance to the idea of leaving home. I remember another loud debate. Anyway, my parents never did send me to Arizona.

There is something heavy about the air in Tangier, even on the hottest and driest days. They say that airplanes slow down as much as forty miles per hour when they pass overhead. Apparently the air is thicker and acts as a brake. I don't know whether to believe that or not; but I do know that, once the rains began, our house never dried out. Patches of grey-green mould began to appear on the walls. The real estate agent had mentioned that it was a summer house. Now I know what he was talking about. From September onwards the house, which faces north and is shaded by tall trees, receives only a few hours of direct sunlight a day. Central heating is unheard of in Tangier, and no room was warm enough for me. I went down to the woodyard, bargained with the woodchoppers over a ton of wood, had it delivered and began to spend most of my time in front of the fireplace.

Alice doesn't seem to mind the damp, but then she is pretty tough. They say the dampness in the walls has to do with the sand they made the cement with when the house was built. Apparently it comes straight off the beach, full of salt, which of course absorbs and retains moisture. The mildew is pretty bad, too. I have to wipe it off my shoes about once a week. What's more I began to have nightmares about mildew.

I had a bad attack just before Halloween. When the doctor arrived I could see he was frightened; and so was I, especially when an intravenous injection had no effect whatsoever. As I began to panic, my lungs tightened up, and I was hardly able to get any air in or out. Luckily a second shot took hold. Gradually the crisis subsided, and I began to breathe normally again. My chest was stiff and sore, like it had been in a vice. Alice said the doctor told her afterwards that it was the worst attack of asthma he had ever seen. Apparently I was turning blue from lack of oxygen.

That worried me. It was the first attack I had had since Alice and I started travelling together. Usually when I am around her I am free of asthma. After the doctor left she rubbed my chest until I fell asleep. Once I receive personal care I tend to recover quickly.

The attacks seem to occur when I am alone in a strange, damp place. What I remember most about them is the feeling of helplessness, of not being able to do anything. When faced with a crisis, I am seized by a certain passivity. I want to believe that things might take a turn for the better, when in fact they are getting worse every minute.

One time in Lima, Peru, I thought my number was up. A thick drizzly mist called the *garua* blankets the city all winter long. This, combined with the pollution produced by thousands of second-hand American cars, makes it the worst possible air for an asthmatic to breathe.

I was all alone and practically suffocating in a shabby little *pensión* on Carabaya. Finally a doctor I had never seen before or since appeared, summoned by a terrified concierge, and gave me a shot which cleared me up. To this day I don't know what was in that syringe, but when he plunged it into my arm I didn't care, so long as it brought relief. Most injections for asthma are powerful heart stimulants. An overdose can bring serious consequences.

In the end I had to be rushed to the hospital. As a result of that experience, cheap hotels inspire a kind of dread in me. I remember every detail of that room in Lima. It was located on the roof, and black vultures roosted on the wall outside my door. They are timid creatures, but the sight of them didn't raise my hopes for a speedy recovery.

I have always been told that I will eventually outgrow my asthma, but I don't believe that any more. If anything, it seems to be getting worse. My nerves become pretty ragged when I can get only two or three hours' sleep a night. Sleeping pills are no help at all. I think I have become immune to stimulants and sedatives, I have taken so many. I suppose I ought to leave Tangier for a drier climate, but there is no place I particularly want to go to. Life can be so pleasant here, aside from the asthma. One of these days they'll discover a miracle drug that will cure me once and for all. I'll just wait.

※

A second attack, which occurred the day we had planned to go to Gibraltar to buy a turkey for Thanksgiving, was less severe; but when it was over Dr Daniels suggested that I recuperate for a few days in his *clinica*, where it is warmer and drier. Alice thought it was a good idea. Poor Alice, she hasn't been feeling too well herself. Says she hasn't any energy when she used to have so much. Probably my being sick has been a strain on her. It's true she hasn't taken any trips lately.

I had been in the *clinica* a few days and was feeling better, when one morning I saw Alice getting out of the car and entering the building. Naturally I was happy, for she hadn't yet visited me. I waited and waited, but she never did come up. I couldn't understand why she had neglected to see me.

As I lay in bed I was reminded of my fifth birthday. I used to spend nearly all my childhood birthdays in the hospital. The excitement of that day almost invariably triggered an asthma attack, so my parties had to be cancelled at the last minute. I remember lying very small in my bed when through the window I saw my mother and father get out of the car and enter the building. I was glad to see them, for I was always lonely in the hospital. I still am. But they never came up either. I spent that birthday by myself in the ward. Later I learned that my sister was born that day. Our birthdays are exactly five years apart.

Alice never did come up. Two days later the doctor said I could go home if I took vitamins regularly and was careful about catching colds, as they can precipitate a crisis. The next time I went swimming, I was to give myself a 'friction,' by rubbing myself all over hard with a rough towel as soon as I came out of the water. This, he said, stimulates the circulation under the skin and reduces the chances of catching a chill. Naturally I intended to follow his instructions; I didn't want any more asthma. I was also anxious to see Alice.

She was not at home. Mohamed handed me a note in which she explained that she had not been feeling well lately, and was going to New York to see a specialist and have a complete physical check-up.

I questioned our Moroccans for details. While I was in the *clinica*, Fatima explained, Alice had started complaining about a bad pain in her stomach. She stayed in bed and didn't touch her food. Her face was pale and she was losing weight. After the visit to Dr Daniels they heard her crying in her room. She made several long telephone calls to the United States before packing a suitcase, not a big one. Mohamed drove her to the airport. She didn't say when she'd be back.

Of course I was worried. But I wasn't sure what to do. Should I jump on the next plane and follow her to New York? Then who would look after the house? She didn't leave any instructions, not even the name of the doctor she was going to see. In the end I decided to wait. I was praying that it would turn out to be nothing serious, for Alice would never take such a trip unless she considered it to be absolutely necessary.

I wandered around the house looking out the windows. It seemed awfully quiet with her gone. Entering her room, I sat down on her bed. Then I lay on it with my hands behind my head. Alice's bed is big and soft. It's an American bed she rented from an ex-rodeo champion from Idaho, who is in the furniture trade in Tangier. Claims he rode with Hoot Gibson. It is covered with a fur rug made from the skins of the *vizcacha*, a Bolivian rodent, that I had brought back from South America.

Bed, Alice maintains, is the best place to drink in. 'Home on the range,' she calls it, raising her glass in a toast. When I brought her her Scotch and soda before going upstairs to my own room, sometimes she beckoned me forward with a finger to her lips, as though someone might be listening. Then she grabbed me. 'I've got you now!' she shouted. 'Guards!' And she pulled the string and the mosquito net cascaded down around us.

By degrees my loneliness faded. I realized I was on my own with a car at my disposal and plenty of time on my hands. I was free to do almost anything I wanted. Besides, Alice would soon be back from New York.

I told Mohamed I wanted to go for a drive. In a minute the car was ready. We drove downtown, where I purchased a couple of hot-water bottles and some vitamin C tablets. Then we took the road that leads to the Atlantic beach.

This is one of the most beautiful beaches in the world. People say it extends all the way to West Africa, thousands of miles to the south. I don't know whether to believe that or not, but it is studded with golden sand dunes and stretches all the way to the horizon, and that is good enough for me. And there isn't a single hot dog wagon which clutter up the American beaches. Although the sun was hot, and the sea blue and smooth, I didn't go in swimming. I had just come out of the *clinica*. Mohamed waited in the car while I walked up and down. The beach was totally deserted, the way a beach ought to be. Seagulls and a herd of cows felt at home out there. I sat down on the side of a sand dune. Looking out across the water, I thought of Alice far away on the other side of the Atlantic and wondered what she must be doing at the same moment. Sleeping, I

guessed, what with the time difference. I became sad
and tried to think of something else, but those
restless birds and the cows wandering aimlessly in
circles just wouldn't let me. As we drove back to
Tangier I was still wondering what could be wrong
with Alice, so far away in America.

That afternoon I wrote a page in my notebook
about the suddenness of solitude and took a nap in
her bed. When I woke the sun was setting. The
fishing boats were on their way back from Cape
Spartel. The rhythmic pulse of their marine engines
makes the windows of our house rattle. I felt in the
mood to sit in front of the fire and write a letter, but
Alice hadn't left a forwarding address. In my address
book I had the telephone numbers of several of her
friends in New York, and debated whether I should
call them or not. I could hear myself saying:

'This is Norman.'

'Hey, Norm! How are you, boy?'

'I'm trying to locate Alice.'

'Last I heard she was living in Morocco.'

'No, no. I'm in Morocco. Alice is in New York.'

'Hey, I thought you two were together.'

'We are.'

'So you haven't split up?'

'No, we haven't, but I don't know where she is.'

That kind of thing. After thinking about it for a
while, I decided not to call. If she had wanted to
keep in touch, surely she would have left a number
where she could be reached.

It was odd the way she went off like that, without

saying a word. It was almost as if she didn't want to tell me goodbye. That's the trouble with being sick yourself. You don't realize until it's too late how ill the person who has been looking after you has been.

✳

The days passed quietly. I began to swim again and lie in the sun. I felt better, except in the evenings, when my asthma acted up because of the damp night air. It's bad enough being alone all day, but when the sun went down I needed someone to talk to. So I took to having my dinners at a restaurant in town and would often go to a bar afterwards for a night-cap, like Alice and I used to do. There are many bars in Tangier, but Alice's favourite is the Chance. The cook is an ex-Wall of Death rider from France and Spain. She knows how to make a decent hamburger. In a paved garden two owls sit side by side in a cage under a palm tree, like a contented elderly couple. I like to carry my drink outside and talk to them.

The bar is owned by an ex-professor of advertising from the University of West Virginia. He's a good friend of Alice. They share a rough-and-ready spirit and laugh at the same kind of jokes. The walls of the bar are hung with red plush curtains, and the lighting fixtures resemble old-fashioned gas lamps with gold reflecting balls. The principal decorations are three large shiny oil paintings depicting half-naked Nubian adolescents rowing Venetian gondolas. An awning projects over the bar, and Tallulah Bankhead's sister's shoes have been nailed to little platforms on either side, so nobody will steal them. The professor takes pride in arranging fresh flowers every day.

The bar is frequented mostly by English and Americans. The Chance is their headquarters.

I took a seat at the end of the bar. The professor came over and poured me a drink.

'When's the old girl coming back from New York?' he asked.

I didn't know, I told him; but soon, I hoped. Alice wasn't so old.

'Cheer up, Norm. She's as tough as nails.'

'She's not as tough as you think.'

The next morning a telegram was delivered to my door. ALICE GRAVELY ILL COME NEW YORK IMMEDIATELY LOIS.

Lois is Alice's sister. I got out my travellers cheques and went down to the airline ticket office and made a reservation for New York. I wanted to leave right away, but the connecting flight to Madrid had already departed, so I had to wait until the next day. The rest of the morning I paced back and forth on the terrace, wondering what could be the matter with Alice. She was so far away and there was nothing I could do. The wind was rising, and I experienced that same feeling of helplessness as when an attack of asthma is impending, and I can see no way of avoiding it or finding relief.

In the afternoon I had Mohamed drive me out to the Atlantic. I didn't enjoy it. The sand dunes had been flattened by storms. The wet beach looked bleak and devoid of life. All I could think of was

Alice out there across the ocean, over which I would be flying the next day. The sun sank into the water without leaving a trace of colour in the sky. For some reason I felt that things were never going to be the same again.

✳

I caught the Iberia flight to Madrid, where I had to wait several hours for the big jet to New York. The minute I boarded it, I knew I was back in the US.

'Hi!' the stewardess said, as though we were all at home. I am not superstitious by nature, but the plane was so big and impersonal, the interior so bland, and the piped music so nauseous that I looked around for some wood to touch, just for good luck.

The stewardess cheerfully assured me that the interior of the plane was made entirely of plastic. Americans can be like that: when unable to meet a serious enquiry they try to make a joke out of it. The passengers laughing and conversing in my own language revived my fears about not being able to cope with this sort of thing.

On the way across the ocean, I read a magazine article about jet lag. Flying across time zones, it said, disrupts the body's biological rhythms, and the system becomes profoundly disorganized. Transatlantic passengers are advised to get plenty of sleep before attending to serious business. 'The business tycoon must never go from the aircraft to the boardroom,' warned Dr Turner. 'Wrong decisions will inevitably be made.'

Since I wasn't a tycoon, I couldn't make my mind

up whether the article applied to me or not. Some business, such as sickness and death, just won't wait, no matter what kind of shape you're in.

I felt uneasy, a sensation that stayed with me after I got off the plane in New York.

From the airport I called several of Alice's friends. To my surprise not one of them knew she was in New York. They asked me to notify them as soon as I had found out where she was staying. I promised I would. Finally her business partner gave me the name of a private clinic on Park Avenue. His voice sounded hoarse. I thought maybe we had a bad connection.

I arrived at the clinic carrying my suitcase. In the reception room two nurses were chatting. One was about my age, I guessed; the other was older, and wore a blue cardigan over her uniform. I came in quietly, so they didn't notice me at first. I had to wait a moment. The bare white walls of the hall reflected the neon light, and the place exuded a hospital smell, with which I was all too familiar. It meant death. Many years ago, the woman in the bed next to mine in the hospital ward hiccupped during the night and died. I knew it before anyone else but didn't say anything because I was too young to be sure. They wheeled her away in the morning. After that the smell was stronger.

The nurses saw me and fell silent.

'Can we help you, sir?'

I explained that I had come to see Alice. The nurses exchanged glances. For a second I thought they didn't believe me, or were wondering what I was doing with a suitcase. I was about to explain that I had just arrived from the airport and hadn't had a chance to leave it anywhere when the older nurse stepped forward. I could see that something was bothering her.

'Are you her son?'

'No, just a good friend.'

'I'm sorry, sir, but Miss Wilson passed away yesterday,' she said.

She made a movement with her hand as if she were going to reach out and touch me, but decided against it. I didn't know what to reply. So I didn't say anything.

'Did you hear me, sir? Miss Wilson passed away yesterday,' she repeated. I could see she was getting uncomfortable. She made another hesitant gesture with her hand, but nothing came of it. My arm was tired from carrying the suitcase.

The nurses looked at each other again.

'Where is she now?' I asked.

'At Universal Funerals,' put in the younger nurse. Her voice was hard. It had an impatient ring to it. I liked the older nurse better.

They gave me Lois's telephone number, as she was Alice's closest relative and was handling the details of the funeral. I called her. The nurses were listening. Lois sounded upset and not very happy to hear the sound of my voice. She and Alice never got on. Once I heard Alice tell her to go to hell and slam down the phone. The conversation had been about me.

The funeral was to be the next day. She gave me

the name and address of the church. When I asked where Alice was, she replied, 'At Universal Funerals.' I didn't ask where that was.

I said goodbye to the nurses, carried my suitcase outside, and hailed a taxi. I told the driver to take me to a hotel, any hotel. Since I'm from New Jersey I've never stayed in a hotel in New York. Usually with friends. He started driving downtown. We passed many hotels along the way, but he didn't stop. I didn't say anything. While we were waiting at an intersection on Lexington Avenue, I looked out the window at a big vertical flashing sign — UNIVERSAL FUNERALS.

I must have walked past the place a dozen times without once suspecting that one day I'd have reason to go inside. Asking the driver to wait, I got out of the taxi and tapped on the door, but it was past five o'clock and the place was shut. The windows were made of tinted glass, through which I could just make out the shadowy forms of potted palms and a number of bulky objects, which I assumed were coffins on display. I was hoping a night watchman or somebody would answer my knock, but all was silent inside. When people on the sidewalk stopped to stare, I stopped banging on the window.

Lexington Avenue teemed with shoppers. The Santa Clauses were ringing their bells and pleading with people to hand over some of their Christmas money for the orphans and the homeless, but it wasn't working. A Salvation Army band played an off-key rendition of 'Silent Night'.

The driver dropped me off at a hotel on 42nd Street. Scott's Hotel, it was called. Transients only. I paid him and carried my suitcase inside. The man behind the desk asked what I wanted.

'A single room,' I replied.

He was eyeing my suitcase. One of the most suspicious objects you can carry around New York nowadays is a suitcase. He didn't seem to have hair anywhere on his body. His head and face had a texture not unlike the bottom of my foot. I almost envied him. I hate shaving.

'All right, that'll be seventy-five dollars. Pay in advance.'

'*Seventy-five dollars?*' I was used to Tangier prices.

'Take it or leave it.'

I paid. He handed me a key.

'Two-fourteen. Second floor. Say, is that all you want? Just a room?'

'That's all, thank you.'

I carried my suitcase upstairs. It was a dreary room with a faded red carpet. A mirror attached to the ceiling above the bed reminded me of a brothel I had once visited in Panama City. But it didn't matter. It was way past my bedtime. I was dog-tired from the trip and had to get up early in the morning.

I conked out right away, then woke up a few hours later, wide awake. I tossed and turned and couldn't get back to sleep. Finally, out of desperation, I took a sleeping pill. That was a mistake, for I didn't wake up again until eleven o'clock. I should have asked the man at the desk to ring me, for the funeral was to have been at ten. At first I was upset, but there was nothing I could do about it. So I stayed in bed another hour. At noon the maid unlocked the door with her own key and announced that I had to vacate the room immediately so she could change the sheets. When I told her that I would probably stay for another night, maybe more, she seemed surprised.

'What? Another night? Haven't you had enough? You men! All right, but you've got to get out of here if you want me to clean the room. I leave in fifteen minutes.'

I shaved as fast as I could and cut myself on a new razor. I have a tough beard. Sometimes I have to shave twice in one day.

That afternoon I called up Lois again. She sounded more annoyed than on the previous night.

'Where were you?' she asked.

'I overslept.'

'Overslept? You have to be kidding!'

I tried to explain that the flight from Tangier had worn me out and that I had forgotten to ask the man at the desk to ring me in the morning. I don't have an alarm clock. I hate them.

When I asked her where Alice was buried, she replied, 'In Queens. Are you serious? You flew all the way over here and slept through the funeral? Christ, I can't believe it!'

She hung up before I could ask where in Queens Alice was buried. I dialled her number back, but the line was busy. I guessed she was calling around town, telling her friends. Later in the day I got hold of her again. She gave me the name and address of the cemetery, but not without asking once more if I had really overslept. She just couldn't seem to believe it. When I assured her that I had, she hung up.

✳

The next day I got into a taxi and asked the driver to take me to Queens. It was a long ride, but I didn't mind. I hadn't been in New York for quite a while, and it gave me a chance to see the sights.

In Queens we passed by huge cemeteries on the left and right. It seemed incredible that so many people had died, and that they were all buried in the same place. The scene gave a hint of the problem the world will have to face in years to come. I'd also heard that this is some of the most valuable real estate in New York.

At last we turned off the highway and drove through a gate. CALVARY – 5 MPH, a sign said. The taxi stopped.

'Will you wait for me?' I asked.

The driver glanced at the meter, which already registered a large sum, and picked up his newspaper.

Inside the gate stood a little white house. A sign sticking out of the grass said CARETAKER. Although automobiles streamed back and forth on the highway just a few yards away, and factory chimneys were belching smoke into the horizon, it was a little like being out in the country.

As I approached the house along a gravel path, a man in an overcoat appeared at the door. I asked him where Alice was buried.

'What's the name?'

'Wilson.'

He went back inside. I stood by the door and watched him open the drawer to one of several large filing cabinets, so large I wondered how they had fitted through the door. Maybe the cottage had been built around them. He thumbed through a mass of cards until he pulled one out. It was whiter than the others. He wrote a number down on a piece of paper and consulted a wallchart. It was covered with little squares. Then he returned to the door.

'Came in yesterday, eh?'

'That's right.'

'Should have said so. That's plot M57.'

He led me outside and pointed up another gravel path.

'You follow that path until you reach another marked M leading off to the right. You take that. It will be grave 57 on the left. You can't miss it. It's fresher than the others. Mother?'

'No, just a good friend.'

He gave me a little shove, and up the path I went. I found path M easily enough but lost count of the graves on my left. I had to go back and start all over again. Had I foreseen how different from the others Alice's grave would be, I wouldn't have bothered. The flowers were fresh, reminding me that I had neglected to bring any; but to my surprise there was no tombstone. I couldn't believe it. Her name was missing, as were the dates of her life. All I had was a number on a scrap of paper. Her body was supposed to be under the ground in a wooden box, but I couldn't even be sure of that for I hadn't actually seen her being placed there. The last time I had seen her was from the window of Dr Daniel's *clinica* in Tangier. I thought she was coming to visit me, and I was wrong about that.

This couldn't be a trick that someone was playing on me. Alice loved practical jokes, but this was carrying things too far. A plot wouldn't be dug up, various people informed, and a funeral staged just for fun. After all, the man in the cottage did have her name on a card.

No, Alice must be dead and lying down there, but I didn't understand how. For a minute I wished I had a shovel to dig her up with, just to make sure. Only a wish, of course; I probably never would have done it.

I wasn't the only one in the cemetery. Other people were wandering the gravel paths, kneeling in front of graves, arranging flowers and straightening little American flags that had become faded and tattered in the wind. It was one of those crystal clear, New York winter days when you can hear people sobbing all around you.

The caretaker assured me that tombstones are never set until months after the burial, so the earth has time to settle.

'Nothing looks more undignified than a fallen

tombstone,' he said, 'or one that isn't standing up straight.'

'People passing on the highway might get the idea that some of the most valuable real estate in the world isn't being properly tended to. Is that another reason?' I wondered.

'That's right. If they saw that this property wasn't being immaculately maintained at all times, pretty soon they'd be wanting it for themselves.'

✳

I hung around New York for a few days. Out of habit, I guess, for I had nothing to do there. As I had been abroad for a long time, the Christmas decorations along Fifth Avenue seemed almost foreign. With Alice gone I couldn't get into the holiday spirit. Besides, I didn't have anyone to buy presents for.

I called my sister in New Jersey. With both our parents dead, she's the only close relative I have left. I told her about Alice, but she didn't offer any condolences. I talked a little about my life in Morocco, and asked if she would like to come and visit, now there was a spare bedroom in the house. She didn't say anything. Fatima made an excellent breakfast, I added, usually eggs fried in olive oil, with Moroccan bread sliced thin and toasted, and strong Arab coffee. If the weather was fine we could go to the beach. Fatima served lunch on the terrace: fresh fish or fresh squid with salad and rosé wine. The first time I saw fried squid on a plate I thought they were onion rings, but now I had got to like them. Mohamed could take us for drives around Tangier. In the evening we could sit around and drink whiskey sours in front of the fire.

'I don't see what that would accomplish,' she said, and put down the phone.

That's the kind of family I come from: people have had their feelings so bruised by divorce they don't want anything to do with each other any more.

I called some friends. Thinking I was in Tangier, they sounded surprised to hear my voice. I said I was going back in a few days and had just called to say hello, to ask how they were. They were fine and wished me a good trip back. One asked me how I was doing at the casino. I think he had Morocco and Monaco confused. Tangier does have a small casino. I've been there once or twice, but only to watch. Alice used to gamble occasionally. I went with her.

Finally, I bought a ticket back to Morocco. I saw no point in sticking around New York any longer. Although I have lived in and around the city most of my life, it didn't feel like home to me. Moreover, I had begun to miss the house in Tangier. I was glad to get on the plane and was not so nervous as before, for I brought along a twig that I had snapped off a bush in Central Park. I kept it in my pocket and touched it from time to time, just for good luck.

Unfortunately, the seat next to mine was occupied by a large woman from Arizona who kept the cold air jet above our heads wide open. It created a terrific draught. As I'm afraid of catching cold, which nearly always leads to more asthma, I asked her to turn it off.

Now I am pretty tall, nearly six feet, although it is true that I don't have very good posture and my chest has expanded from years of coughing; but this woman towered over me.

'Take your choice,' she said in a gruff voice. 'Air, or do you want me to be sick in your lap? Big fellow like you ought to be warm enough.'

If my parents had sent me out west, cold air might not have affected my breathing. On the other hand, maybe it was just as well they hadn't. I couldn't possibly have competed with a woman of this breed. Probably she ran a big spread in Arizona single-handed. My ranch would have been a flop.

I told her I would take my chances. Reluctantly she turned off the air, but not without mumbling something under her breath. I thought I heard the word 'dude.' Later I lit a cigarette. She ordered me to stop blowing smoke in her face, which I was not doing, and threatened to vomit then and there. To avoid further difficulties I ground out the cigarette. Afterwards I became angry with myself for not standing up to her. If Alice had been there, she would have put the woman in her place.

✳

It was already dark by the time the connecting flight from Madrid landed in Tangier. At the airport a breeze was blowing. The shiny palmettos shivered under the spotlights. It had been raining. A taxi driver, who seemed to know me, offered to take me into town for half the regular fare, since we were friends. Naturally, I accepted. After being on my own in New York, I was glad to have someone recognize me. He seemed happy that I had returned to Tangier, and so was I.

He asked how my trip was. As I saw no point in telling him about Alice, I said that it had been fine.

'But it's always good to come back to Tangier, no?'

As his was the first friendly voice I'd heard in several days, I had to agree with him.

On the way into town he rattled on about the virtues of Tangier. Did I know why Tangerines have no wrinkles? And why is it that everyone who leaves eventually returns, as though drawn by a magnet? And why, as soon as they arrive, do they begin to breathe easier?

My mind had been wandering, trying to imagine what life in Tangier would be like without Alice; I couldn't come up with any answers.

'Because, my friend, all Tangerines — and that includes Americans like you and Moroccans like me — the English people and the Spanish people and the Arabic people, even the Jews — people who in other parts of the world would be fighting day and night — here in Tangier they all agree on one subject.'

'What's that?'

'That there's no place in the world like Tangier. The other day I picked up some Spanish friends in the port. They had left Tangier because there was no work, and swore they'd never come back again.

They went to the Costa de Sol, where everything is new and ugly. They went to Madrid, which is so noisy they couldn't hear themselves think. They went to Barcelona, where there are so many cars they were afraid to cross the street. They came to the conclusion that people who inhabit the so-called civilized world are living like savages and don't even know it. My friends are back in Tangier for good now, and swear they'll stay for the rest of their lives, even if they have to beg for a living.'

It was a cheerful logic expressed by a man with black skin and square white teeth. That's one reason I like countries like Peru and Morocco. People have to work day and night to make ends meet, they don't have much, but when they greet you it's with a smile that makes you stop and count your blessings. Just to hear his welcoming words made me glad I was back.

'Yes, sir. In Tangier you meet some very odd people living under the same roof. People who otherwise might be snarling at each other like beasts go to the beach hand in hand. Dogs and cats eat out of the same bowl...'

On the way up the Old Mountain, he inhaled deeply and declared with conviction that of all the people who make their homes in Tangier, those who live on the Old Mountain are the luckiest.

'Look at all these eucalyptus and pine trees! Everybody knows that eucalyptus oil is good for the nose and throat. And the pine trees filter the sea air, and sea air filtered by pine trees preserves the complexion and is best for breathing. All the doctors say so. It's the only subject they can agree on.'

When the taxi pulled up in front of the house, Fatima and Mohamed rushed out to greet me. There was nearly a tug of war over who was going to carry my suitcase.

'Now tell me, my friend,' observed the taxi driver as he pocketed the fare, 'where else in the world are you going to get a reception like this?'

Mohamed and Fatima were so overjoyed to have me home that I was reluctant to tell them about Alice. I hate scenes or loud noises of any kind. Before the divorce my parents used to scream at each other. It was like listening to wild animals being eviscerated. I used to dread those fights with doors slamming and things breaking. I buried my head under the pillow or went into hiding with my hands over my ears. My little sister lay in the next bedroom. One can only guess whether those shouting voices penetrated the subconscious of the sleeping child; whether she was already beginning to experience that primeval insecurity when the ground shakes, and the world she considered secure begins to crack and split beneath her feet.

When I couldn't stand it any longer, I would run into the kitchen and stand between them like the referee in a heavyweight boxing match. But it didn't stop the fights. Afterwards my mother used to creep into my bedroom, press her tear-stained cheek to mine, and ask if I still loved her. How else could my heart respond but more desperately than ever? As a result, violent emotions upset me.

Well, Fatima and Mohamed began asking about Alice, and I had to tell them. At first there was silence, as though they didn't believe me. Fatima ran away into the kitchen, where I could hear her sobbing. Then she rushed back into my arms. It's awkward hugging your maid, but sometimes there isn't anyone else. Mohamed was trying to be manly. He gripped my shoulder and told me what a good woman she was. How kind and generous. All the Moroccans thought so. God would reward her by placing her in the best part of women's heaven.

While all this was going on around me, like winds blowing away veils, I realized for the first time that she was truly dead. In New York I had been assured that it was so; but it took the sight of tears and the sound of hoarse and muffled cries to convince me she was gone forever. It was the end of an era, and the Moroccans had understood it more quickly than I had. I went into her room and lay down on the bed while the house grew silent.

When I came out, Mohamed had disappeared. I guessed he had gone to tell his friends. Fatima was still moaning in the kitchen.

As I didn't have the heart to ask her to cook supper, I telephoned a taxi and went into town. Unconsciously resuming my old ways, I wandered into the Chance bar, where I was greeted on all sides. The professor shook my hand and poured me a drink. A gravelly voice down the bar asked how Alice was. I replied that she was dead. At first they thought I was joking. Someone laughed. But when I told them that I had been to the clinic, talked to the nurses and, although I had slept through the funeral, had visited the cemetery in Queens and seen her grave, fresh flowers and all, they began to believe me.

The professor, however, could not resist leaning over and asking me in a confidential tone of voice which could be heard by everyone in the bar:

'You mean to say, Norm, that after going all that way, you actually slept late and missed the funeral?'

There was silence. People gave me strange looks that made me feel uncomfortable.

I tried to remember that article about jet lag, and explained that the trip from Tangier had exhausted me. The plane had arrived late and I had forgotten to ask the man at the desk to ring me; but it didn't seem to make much of an impression.

Just then the ex-Wall of Death rider poked her nose out of the kitchen.

'I don't blame you, kid,' she croaked. 'When my old man popped off, I didn't make it to the funeral, either. I ain't even seen where he's buried.'

Most of that night I sat on the edge of the bed holding my head in my hands, wheezing and coughing out my lungs. The next morning I was so exhausted I stayed under the covers. Fatima brought me coffee. Her eyes were still red from crying.

I had visited Fatima's home the day I lent her the parrot to amuse her mother who had had a stroke. The house was inhabited, as far as I could see, solely by women. They sat around making cakes and cookies, banging on drums and singing. Each time the parrot whistled, a goofy, toothless smile spread across the old lady's face. Everybody has problems but, in a group like that, each did her best to cheer the others up. I would have never guessed that Fatima's household was beset by sorrows, when in fact there were many. The Moroccans understand that during hard times people should stick together, make cakes and sing. That way the pain is shared and nobody is left out.

As the east wind was blowing hard, rattling the shutters, I stayed in Alice's room, looking at her things. Her room is the driest in the house. Lying on her bed, I wondered what life would be like without her. I didn't know exactly, except that it would be completely different from the one that was just ending. One thing was certain: someone different from the person I had been would be needed to survive in it.

I was still not one hundred per cent convinced that Alice was dead, but if she truly was, as the nurses at the clinic had assured me, then I must not think about her all the time, but try to set out to lead a life independent of her and her memory. Of course, there was nothing wrong about thinking of her from time to time, which is only natural, but I could not live on that memory alone.

✳

I did not see any reason for leaving Tangier. I had the house and the car and an established pattern of living that need not be abandoned. There was

Fatima to do the cooking, and Mohamed to drive the
car and keep the garden in order. I had enough
money to keep me going for a while. When that ran
out I could always sell the car, which Alice had
placed in my name. Perhaps she had foreseen that I
might want to do that one day. Alice was like that:
she would do things for me without telling me. For
example, one day I was rummaging in the glove
compartment of the car and noticed that the registra-
tion was in my name. I asked her why.

'In case you want to take off one day, now you've
got wheels,' she said.

I told her I never thought of taking off and, even
if I did, I had never owned a car and didn't know
how to drive one properly.

'Forget it,' she replied, and wouldn't say another
word about it.

I worked on my notebook for a while, putting
down the events of the last few days, so I could keep
them straight in my head. Afterwards I weighed the
possibilities of what I might do in the evening. I
could read a book, but that meant spending more
time in bed. Or, I could have supper and a drink at
the Chance, but I didn't feel like talking to those bar
people again. Or, I could go to the movies, but in
Tangier most of the films have been dubbed into
French or Arabic, and I don't speak either language
well enough to understand.

It was a pity Alice had died. She always had
plenty of ideas. Sometimes she would come out onto
the terrace and say:

'Come on, lazy, roll out of that hammock! What are you writing – a goddamn newspaper? Let's go for a drive!'

Alice was always a little jealous of my diary. I had started keeping it in South America, when I didn't have anyone to talk to. Now that it had become a habit, she seemed to look upon my notebook like it was another person living in the house with us, a rival who I communed with regularly, on a private basis, excluding her.

I took the gin bottle out of the fridge, mixed up a batch of really cold martinis, poured them into a thermos bottle, and off we went. We never told Mohamed which direction to take, but it didn't make any difference. Pretty soon we would be tight and laughing, and making Mohamed laugh, too. He would laugh louder than anyone, even though he hadn't had a drop to drink, and couldn't understand a word we said. He nearly drove off the road a couple of times, but we went slowly so there was no real danger. Alice swore at him, which made him laugh all the harder. She used some pretty colourful swear words, fancy but not mean.

We used to do that about once a month. One time we went all the way to Tetuan, about an hour away. All the martinis had been drunk, so we stopped at a Spanish café for a refill. Sawdust covered the floor and old bullfight posters adorned the walls. Thermos in hand, Alice marched behind the bar and mixed up another batch for the trip home. The bartender just stood aside in amazement. When Alice strides forward, head down, with that determined look on her face, people sensibly get out of the way. A drunk at the bar was waving his jacket like a bull fighter and shouting, *'Olé!'*

We drove across the Moroccan countryside drinking martinis and singing 'Onward Christian Soldiers'. By the time we got back to Tangier, we were really high. I remember sitting in the back seat with Alice, feeling warm and happy. Then for some reason she stopped talking and looked at me in a strange way, as though some unpleasant thought had suddenly occurred to her, spoiling the occasion. When I asked her what was the matter, she told me to shut up, so I did. Maybe the gin had put her in a bad mood. You can't get English gin in Tetuan, only the Spanish kind. The bottles are identical, the labels look alike, but it doesn't taste the same.

✳

Tangier is definitely not the same without Alice. Frankly, I didn't know what to do with myself, so I stayed at home most of the time. Once again I felt the need to find a job, not just for the money, but mainly to have something to do.

One position I had my eye on was already held by an old man who lived down the road. He was the night watchman for a large wooded property whose owners seemed to be permanently absent.

Carrying a club and a basket, he arrived with his dog around dusk at a shack he had built against the trunk of a eucalyptus tree. The first thing he did was to feed the dog with the food he had brought in the basket. Then he made a fire and put on a kettle. He wore an orange turban wrapped tightly about his head, and a brown djellaba. On his feet were pointed yellow leather slippers.

By the time the water was boiling, his friends, a fisherman returning from the coast and a woodchopper from the forest, turned up for tea. Then the old man made supper. The fisherman might contribute a fish to the pot, and the woodsman brought something from the forest, like mushrooms or pine nuts. Many times I used to come home with Alice late at night and see them beneath the boughs of the eucalyptus tree, smoking and chatting, their faces lit by the glow of the fire. What with the leafy branches of the tree just overhead, and the knobbly roots that served as natural benches and stools, it looked like a cosy place to spend the night.

I would have bet anything that their conversation was more interesting than the gossip I'd had to listen to in the bars. I never said so to Alice, but this seemed a worthy occupation – to sit up late and keep watch while the rest of the world slept. As I happen to be an habitually light sleeper, it never takes much to keep me awake night after night. This line of work seemed ideally suited for me.

At least I had Fatima and Mohamed as companions. It's reassuring to know there's someone else in the house, someone to talk to even if it's only to discuss the weather. Of course, Mohamed drives me out to the Atlantic whenever I want, but after a while I grew less fond of that deserted beach. Sometimes I saw a couple walking hand in hand, or a family swimming out there and enjoying the sun. I envied them. I couldn't help it. I guess what I wanted more than anything else was company.

As the weather turned cold and rainy my asthma grew worse, and in the end became almost continuous. I was spending most days in bed, gradually growing immune to the large quantities of medicine that Dr Daniels prescribed. Finally he confessed that any treatment is hopeless in a place like Tangier. The winter climate is too damp for anyone with a chronic respiratory complaint, especially when aggravated by emotional strain. He advised me to leave town for a while, go on a trip to the south of Morocco, where the weather is warmer and the air drier, and to leave my melancholy associations behind.

Although I agreed with him in principle, the idea of leaving Tangier didn't appeal to me at all, especially with Christmas coming on. I had already travelled around Morocco with Alice, and had spent more time longing to return to Tangier than taking in the sights.

'Get on the stick, will you!' she used to say. 'We'll be back in Tangier soon enough. You're in Marrakesh now (or Fez, or wherever we happened to be) so you better take a good look. In a few years it's all going to disappear.'

What with all those children running around loose, to me it looked like more of the same thing to come. I tried to work up an interest, but our house in Tangier was always in the back of my mind. I believe Alice was happiest in Tangier, too, but she had more energy than I do and forced herself to explore every place we visited, except the Sahara. The desert didn't interest her and may have even frightened her, but I could have stayed longer. Now the thought about going back to Zagora and recuperating there occurred to me, but in the end I decided against it. The desert environment might prove to be too harsh to cope with when I was missing someone and not feeling very strong.

✳

Instead of letting Mohamed drive, I decided to try hitch-hiking for a change, and save money on gas. So I put a few things into a suitcase and asked him to drop me off on the road outside Tangier.

I had never hitch-hiked before, but had seen other people do it. At first I was surprised that no one stopped. Alice and I used to pick up hitch-hikers occasionally; it had never occurred to me there would be any difficulty in obtaining a ride. I stuck out my thumb, but nothing happened. Perhaps I wasn't doing it properly, for the cars continued to whiz by. I waited several hours and had almost given up hope, when a little white car travelling very fast slammed on its brakes and skidded to a halt up ahead. I ran after it. A woman opened the door and asked in English where I was going.

'Marrakesh,' I said breathlessly and tried to get in.

'Wait!' she said. 'What about that?'

She was pointing down the road. My suitcase. I had completely forgotten my suitcase and had to run back

45

to get it. When I finally squeezed into the car, she said they were going to Casablanca, about half-way.

It was so cramped in the back seat that I had to hold the suitcase on my knees. But I was grateful to be moving at last. Suddenly, I liked hitch-hiking. It became an adventure when someone stopped.

The man, a Moroccan with a wrinkled forehead and deep-set eyes, drove very fast. I tried not to notice. She was English, with reddish hair, freckles and an interesting gap between her two front teeth. She seemed happy to have someone to talk to, and so was I. She said they lived in Tangier and were going to Casablanca on business. She asked me a lot of questions. I told her I was going to Marrakesh for health purposes but wasn't looking forward to it. I had no friends there, or anything to do, except breathe the dry air.

'Oh,' she exclaimed, 'I know exactly what you mean! When I first came to Tangier I thought I would go mad. Hamid here was working all the time. I didn't know anyone and just stayed at home. I was so lonely and bored! Whenever a Arab woman walked by the house – I used to sit by the window, like a cat – I wanted to run out and give her a hug and invite her in for a cup of tea. Just to have someone to talk to! Our house had just been white-washed, and whenever it rained I dashed outside with a brush and scrubbed the paint that had been spilled on the drive. Down on my hands and knees I was, out in the pouring rain! Wore out the brush completely. Rubbed each bristle down to a nub and just to have something to do. Isn't that crazy? Oh, I was frantic with boredom, I was.'

She was a lively girl with soft-looking breasts that swayed back and forth when she moved. When she talked, a little bubble formed in that gap between her two front teeth, popped, and formed again. I liked to watch it. Every now and then she would lean over and give her husband a kiss on the cheek. Each time she did that he jammed his foot down on the accelerator, and the little car zoomed ahead even faster. He seemed to enjoy her kisses so much that I secretly wished she would give me one, too. The last person to kiss me was Alice, the day she bundled me off to the *clinica*.

'Hamid is mad about gardening. A horticulturist, he calls himself,' she said good-naturedly. She turned half-way around in her seat so she had both of us as her audience. 'We had melons last summer, didn't we, Hamid? Oh, you should have seen our melons! Yellow ones they were, and every night, around midnight, he took the electric torch and went out into the garden in his pyjamas and picked little worms off his melons, one by one.' The bubble went pop. 'Didn't you, dear?' she added.

Hamid soberly replied that the worms came out only at night and otherwise would have eaten the melons. She laughed, planted another kiss on his cheek and hugged him as well.

I sort of flinched when she did that and gave my suitcase a squeeze. I couldn't help feeling a bit lonely. They were in the front seat where they could

kiss and hug, while I was in the back with only a
suitcase on my knees. I'd read somewhere that
couples are happier than people who live alone.
They live longer, too.

We got to Casablanca in about five hours. She
invited me to join them for supper but I declined,
seeing that her husband wanted to be alone with her.

After saying goodbye, I walked past a series of
makeshift foodstalls that had been set up on the
street, offering things like sheep's heads, stuffed
camel intestines and blackened cows' hooves. Finally
I stopped before a fellow grilling lamb kebabs over a
charcoal brazier. When the kebabs were cooked, he
cut a loaf of flat Moroccan bread in two, sliced it
down the middle and drew the kebab sticks through
it, pulling off the meat. He sprinkled on a little coarse
salt mixed with cumin and handed me the sandwich
wrapped in a paper napkin. I'd never tasted anything
better.

Cheap hotel rooms are an ordeal for me. If you
have someone to share it with, any accommodation,
no matter how shabby, becomes a challenge and an
adventure; but when you are alone, drab surround-
ings just seem to deepen your sense of isolation.

The bed was lumpy, and the mattress sagged in
the middle. I scratched all night. The next morning
my ankles were covered with red bites. Bedbugs, I
supposed. Casablanca is a big city. As I didn't know
where to start hitch-hiking, I caught a bus to
Marrakesh.

✳

When Alice and I visited Marrakesh, we stayed in a big, expensive hotel called the Mamounia, located just inside the old city walls. They say that Winston Churchill used to stay there when he came to Morocco after the war to paint, soak up the sun and write his memoirs. As I don't paint and am not surrounded by people interested in keeping me happy like such a famous man as Mr Churchill, I decided to stay somewhere else.

There was also the question of the pocket-book. With Alice gone, I was operating on a limited budget. I planned not to spend much money in the south of Morocco.

I didn't know exactly where to look, for I am not familiar with Marrakesh. It's a deceptively big city, full of narrow winding alleys guaranteed to confuse New Yorkers. However, I finally discovered a little hotel not far from the Mamounia, located on a wide, American-style street. The rear entrance gave onto the Arab quarter, so I had a choice, if it ever came to that. Bedbugs were probably hiding in the sheets, but I was too tired to look any further.

Actually, the room they gave me wasn't all that bad. It had its own bathroom, with a sink and toilet that worked, and a view of the mountains. The shower only let out a little trickle of water. I unpacked my suitcase and spread my possessions around, making the place mine. Unscrewing the showerhead, with my pen knife I gouged out the holes that had become encrusted with limescale. After that it produced a strong spray. I went out and bought toilet paper and soap and some lemons, which I placed in a bowl on the table by the window, for colour.

I spent exactly one week in Marrakesh. All seven of those days were more or less the same. In the morning I hired one of those horse-drawn carriages, like the ones they have in Central Park, only much cheaper, of course. I had the same carriage and driver every day. He came to my hotel at any hour I desired, which was convenient. His name was Moktar. We drove all over the city and outside, too, through the oasis where cows and sheep graze peacefully under the olive trees. We went practically everywhere a horse-drawn carriage can go. I enjoyed it. A horse-drawn carriage travels at a speed that suits me perfectly. It allowed me to take in the sights without being pestered by the children.

At lunchtime Moktar dropped me off at one of the French restaurants in the European part of town. The food was nearly always good, but I don't like to eat alone. I prefer to share a meal with someone else, and to talk and to laugh, rather than pretend to read a newspaper or gaze furtively at the other diners, wishing I were with them. But many times one does not have a choice in such matters.

After lunch I always took a long siesta, often lasting to early evening. I would get up and wander about the town on foot, sometimes stopping at a café for a glass of mint tea and to jot down a few words in my notebook. Little descriptions, like the way lovers hold hands in the park. Or how the sight of a white egret pecking the ticks off a cow's back made me envy the cow because it reminded me of the back rubs Alice used to give me when I was sick. Or the way a dust devil hisses across an empty lot, sucking dust into the crystal air before expiring with a sigh like the soul of one who has vanished and departed. Fleeting observations you might forget two minutes later if you didn't write them down.

Then I walked to the Djemaa el Fna for snails. I got to like snails in Paris because Alice used to order them. Moroccan snails are smaller than the French ones, and they live in white shells decorated with brown stripes. In Marrakesh they are served by ambulatory vendors who wheel bubbling cauldrons along on a kind of tricycle. They ladle the snails into clay bowls along with the herbal brew they are cooked in. Safety pins stuck in an orange are provided to pick them out of their shells with. You are expected to drink the brew afterwards.

The snail man in his white robe and skull-cap got used to seeing me every day. I became one of his regular customers. He assured me that if I continued to eat snails my breathing would improve. By way of illustration, he told me a story about a rich man who suffered from a supposedly incurable back ailment.

Putting down his ladle, he mimed a man who went about with a walking-stick one foot long. His forehead almost bumped along the ground, so bent over was he. The best doctors in France and Belgium were unable to cure him. Then one day a local medicine man advised him to eat snails. By degrees his posture improved, and he bought a longer stick. After many snails he threw it away and stood erect.

If you don't stand up straight, the snail man counselled me, the stomach presses against the lungs. That's why I don't breathe properly. And the lungs press against the heart, which already has enough to do. His advice was to eat more snails, and I would eventually be cured.

Marrakesh is a beautiful city, I decided, all spread out. The buildings have been painted various shades of dull red, like the colour of the earth. The avenues are planted with orange trees whose fragrant blossoms lure lovers into the parks at night. Bitter orange trees, Moktar pointed out, so the children won't steal the fruit. The wide main street and low buildings of the European quarter reminded me a little of American cow towns out west. That's where I felt most at home.

I had my dinner late, like Alice and I used to in Spain. I was always the last customer to leave. Anything to postpone the reality of returning alone to my hotel room. The Moroccan waiters clustered about my table to ask questions about jobs in America. The wages are a lot higher than they are in Morocco, I told them, but so are the prices. They're better off where they are, surrounded by family and friends.

At night I read for as long as I could stay awake, sometimes copying into my diary a passage containing a truth or an idea I didn't want to forget, and always slept late in the morning. When I opened the shutters the cool air and warm sunlight flowed in, and there was Moktar, perched on his carriage, waving and waiting. It wasn't so bad, really. Moreover I was practically free of asthma, so I couldn't complain too much.

One evening Moktar invited me to his home for supper and presented me to his wives. One was a diminutive, tattooed Berber woman from the Atlas Mountains, as white as any English lady, but oriental-looking nevertheless. The other was a broad-shouldered Saharan girl from the River Dra, with scars for decorations. During supper Moktar explained how the women took turns. On alternating nights one or the other prepared his food and shared his bed. The Saharan girl specialized in hot, spicy dishes which made me sweat. According to Moktar, the Berber woman used a lot of milk in her recipes. The system must have worked, for they were all happy and smiling. What I had read about couples being happier must have applied to them as well. The Berber woman proudly showed me her little white baby, and the Saharan girl was bouncing a brown one on her knee. They both wanted to know how many wives and children I had. When I confessed I didn't have any, the conversation came to a stop. Moktar came to my defence by pointing out that a young man likes to travel and have adventures before settling down. On this there was general agreement.

✳

The Atlas Mountains began to interest me. Gleaming with snow, they are seldom out of sight from

Marrakesh. I contemplated taking a short excursion up into them. I knew from Peru that mountain air is good for breathing. And before a cure was found for tuberculosis, they used to have sanatoriums up in the Swiss Alps, where consumptive people could go and sometimes be cured by breathing the pure mountain air. I was reading a novel about it. The hero got to like the sanatorium so much that he didn't want to leave for any reason, and he wasn't even sick.

I thought I would do the same, only for asthma. I doubted they had any sanatoriums in the Atlas Mountains, but I could look around on my own. In the hotel they were mounting decorations for the Christmas revel, which I wished by all means to avoid.

I decided to leave the day before Christmas but wasn't able to cash a travellers cheque, because the banks closed early. After I paid the bill at the hotel, I discovered that I had left only a hundred dirhams, or about twenty American dollars. But that didn't worry me. They say that life is cheap up in the Atlas Mountains. You can live on practically nothing. I intended to go up there to breathe the air and probably wouldn't spend much money. Before setting out I spent twenty-five dirhams on a copy of *Time* magazine. I thought I might want to keep up with current events while travelling far from civilization.

I waited on the road outside Marrakesh for about an hour without getting a lift. It was a warm, sunny day, and I sat on a kilometer stone and read an article in *Time* about the wars that were going on over Christmas in various parts of the world. Only two trucks and three cars went by in my direction. Also, a flock of sheep filtered by. The shepherd was dressed in animal skins that gave off a powerful odour. Pointing at the photograph of a US marine on the cover of *Time*, he made me understand that the Moroccans could defeat the American army, even with all its tanks and airplanes. Pulling out a knife, he showed me how they would do it. His concept of warfare meant sneaking up and killing an enemy soldier 'hilal-style,' by slitting his throat. Holding up the imaginary head of an American marine, he yelped with triumphant laughter. I don't think he'd heard of the A-bomb.

His sheep had scattered. While he shouted and threw stones, I picked up my suitcase and began to walk. The suitcase was not heavy, although it had inside a new Moroccan blanket I had just bought. Winter nights in Marrakesh can be chilly, and I thought it might come in handy up in the mountains. Shifting the suitcase from hand to hand, I passed eight kilometer stones along the road. That's five miles, about the farthest I had ever walked in my life, and I wasn't even tired.

Finally a truck stopped. The driver was a sociable fellow who was taking a load of tangerines over the mountains. He gave me one, which I peeled and ate. I like tangerines. Some people say Tangier gave its name to the fruit, and the inhabitants of Tangier are also known as Tangerines. I tried to explain this to the driver. He nodded and smiled, but I don't think he understood. One problem was that in French, the language in which we were attempting to conduct this conversation, tangerines go by the names of *mandarines*. Neither of us spoke much French, but it was a pleasant ride. I began to appreciate a truck's good points. You sit up high, and there's a big window to look through. Moroccan trucks don't go fast, but they are solid and secure.

The driver dropped me off in a town called Asni, some forty-five kilometers from Marrakesh, where in the market square I bought for another twenty-five dirhams a paper bag full of warm hard-boiled eggs, salt to eat them with, some more tangerines and a supply of macaroons. Tapping an egg on the edge of my suitcase, I spotted Jebel Toubkal in the distance. This is the tallest peak in the Atlas Mountains, some 14,000 feet high. On my map I picked out a little town at its base called Imlil, some seventeen kilometers from Asni. A dotted line looked like a track. Although it was already late in the afternoon, I resolved to make Imlil my final destination for the day. Asni, after all, isn't really in the mountains. It is just surrounded by hills.

As I walked along the sun began to go down, and the snowy flanks of Jebel Toubkal turned pink, then orange, then purple. The track paralleled a roaring river. The minute the sun set, the temperature dropped by several degrees. The moon made an appearance. I detected a little vegetation along the trail – a few stunted trees and bushes hanging on for dear life among the sliding rocks and mud. You have to be resourceful to survive in the mountains, and I wasn't sure I was up to it. After a while I began to pass patches of snow, which glowed like milk in the moonlight. It was spooky but exciting. Every kilometer or so I put my suitcase down and rested. My arms were tired and my hands were cold. The lights of Asni twinkled in the valley below me. They looked warm and inviting. I hoped I was doing the right thing.

After about four hours I spied a light up ahead, and a few minutes later I entered Imlil. It was a tiny hamlet consisting, so far as I could make out in the dark, of two rows of stone huts along a street that lay deep in snow. Chances were I wouldn't find a hotel here, let alone a sanatorium, but then I didn't have much money.

The village dogs assembled to bark, but otherwise it appeared that the entire population of Imlil had retired for the night. I put my suitcase down in the snow, threw snowballs to keep the snarling dogs at bay, and waited. Finally some goats came by with bells clanking, followed by a man in a djellaba. Some other men gathered to stare. It was impossible to make out their faces, which the hoods of their djellabas cast in deep shadow. No one said a word. In the silence of our group, the dogs could be heard howling all over the mountains as they spread the news of my arrival.

Finally I said *bonsoir*. Out of the darkness came a similar reply. We got on a little in French. I opened a pack of cigarettes, distributed them around, and we all had a smoke. As the cigarettes were lit I got a glimpse of their faces. Like our American Indians, I thought, with ruddy skin and high cheekbones. These fellows were Berbers, another racially pure group. I said I was American. This was translated for the benefit of the others. At that they all began to talk at once. I asked if there was a hotel in their village. That made them laugh. One offered me a place to sleep in his house, for fifty dirhams. But that was all the money I had, I said. This was translated for the others and evoked a murmur of astonishment. No doubt they considered all Americans to be fabulously rich, which doesn't surprise me, the way I have seen our tourists throwing their money around. I didn't attempt to explain that the banks were closed and I couldn't cash a travellers cheque.

So I said good-night and carried my suitcase to the edge of the village, hoping to find a barn or haystack to sleep in. Here again I was lucky, for I came across a manure pile, which gives out heat of its own and had melted the snow. I could see the vapour rising in the moonlight. The smell was pretty strong, but I didn't let it put me off. I was more interested in keeping warm.

I put on all my clothes – two extra pairs of socks on my feet and one on my hands, two pairs of trousers and two sweaters. I rolled up in my blanket and wrapped my scarf around my head, like a turban. I had heard that, when sleeping outdoors, if you keep your head covered, the rest of your body will stay warm. I lay on my back in the manure and looked up at the stars, which were unusually bright and numerous in spite of the moon. It was very still and icy cold. In a ghostly universe that rang with silence, somewhere a dog began to bark. It was a short, persistent yap which never seemed to let up.

As I lay there I remembered it was Christmas Eve. A year ago Alice and I had been in New York together. She had gone out to celebrate with some friends. I hadn't felt up to it and had stayed home watching TV. Something disagreeable must have happened at the party, for she came home drunk and angry. She yelled and slammed the doors, which she knows I don't like. I got up and asked her not to do that. She quieted down, mixed herself a night-cap and went off to bed. In the silence that followed I lay awake listening to her snore. After a bout of drinking, Alice really sawed wood.

The next morning we exchanged presents. I gave her a necklace of pre-Columbian beads I'd been keeping in reserve, and she gave me a pair of silver hairbrushes with my initials engraved on the backs. For some reason that memory made my nose run, and my eyes filled with tears. They came out hot and froze on my cheeks.

After drifting off to sleep I woke an hour later shaking with cold. The icy air had penetrated the lower end of the blanket. I tried putting on my shoes, but they wouldn't fit over the socks. I drew in my feet, thrust my hands between my knees, and tried breathing down into the blanket, but to no avail.

This theory about keeping your head warm at night didn't work for me. My body heat was just no match for the cold of the Atlas Mountains. Finally I burrowed deeper into the manure and felt a little more comfortable.

The moon, trailed by its little companion Venus, had sailed across the sky. The hour was approaching midnight. All over the world people were celebrating, or were waiting for Santa Claus to come. I paid attention to the night but heard no sound. I wished that dog, whose bark I had found irritating earlier, would start up again. Anything. The stillness was chilling and powerful. I became frightened, not of the dark and silence, or of the wolves and lynxes I had been told inhabited the mountains, but of the future. It just didn't seem to hold out much promise.

❋

Although I must have dozed from time to time, I spent most of the night shivering and fearful that my asthma would return. Surprisingly enough, it didn't. Maybe it was just as well I couldn't sleep. If you're caught out in the snow, sleepiness is the first sign that you're freezing to death. So I've heard. At first light I crawled out of the manure. The air was bitterly cold, and I jumped up and down on the snow to warm myself. The effort nearly made me faint from breathlessness, so I stopped. I ate two eggs and all the cookies and wished I'd bought more food in Asni. With the sun coming up behind the mountains I noted on the map that Imlil is 6,000 feet above sea level.

Jebel Toubkal was hidden by lesser peaks. As I wanted a closer look, I rolled up my blanket, picked up my suitcase and set out on a path where the snow had been trodden down. After a while the climbing became too steep to proceed. The rocky terrain was blanketed with deep snow. My feet were cold, but the snow was dry and crunchy, and the sun warmed my back a little. The sky was dark blue, almost black, and the white mountains glistened. I felt like a speck in a black and white photograph. I decided that, after all, I had done the right thing to come to the mountains for Christmas. If I'd stayed in Marrakesh, I'd probably be so hung-over that the sight of these pristine slopes would seem unbearable. I clambered onto a boulder, brushed away the cushion of snow, and sat down. I really hadn't planned on going any farther.

I removed my socks and loafers and let them dry out. The sun had become so warm that I was able to shed my blazer, loosen my necktie, and roll up my shirtsleeves. Adjusting my dark glasses, I daubed some cream on my nose and sunbathed a bit. I wrote a description of the scene in my diary and ate all the tangerines. They tasted good and I wished I'd brought more food along.

My nose began to twitch; there was smoke in the air. In a gorge below me, down which the water rushed in a series of alarming spouts and waterfalls, I spotted a shack nestled among the boulders. After wading through snow up to my knees I was greeted by an elf of a man in a tattered djellaba. He didn't act in the least surprised when I bounded out of a drift, covered with snow. He went on sitting in the sun, repairing his boots with a curved needle and heavy thread. A flock of ugly black ravens was sitting on the snow, making hoarse grunting sounds.

While we shared my cigarettes I noticed that his smoky hut was in reality a store. For two dirhams I purchased a can of sardines, which I pried open with my penknife and ate on the spot. I was famished. A green flag was flying from a small, white-domed building which I hadn't noticed before, because it was the same colour as the snow. Through holes in the man's djellaba a green undergarment was visible. Green, Mohamed had told me, is Allah's colour. It is also the colour of hope.

The man's chapped cheeks were creased like old wrapping paper, and wrinkles converged on two bright blue eyes. In a high-pitched, scratchy voice punctuated by peeps and whistles, as though his wind-pipe were leaking, he explained that he was the guardian of the domed building, which he called a *koubba*, or tomb where a holy man is buried.

He showed me around inside, which was spotless and hospital-like. He had painted the interior walls a kind of cool blue, so it was a little like being under water. Bugs don't like blue, he said. The colour went nicely with the green and yellow tiles of the tomb. A pile of sheepskins was his bed. There was a box for his boots and clothes, and a shelf for his paintbrushes and tools. He had a lantern and a supply of candles. His prayer rug was rolled up in the corner. He did his cooking outside over a Bunsen burner. He had everything he needed. The icebox was the great outdoors, and so was the toilet. A couple of potted plants stood in the sunshine by the door: basil to keep the flies away, coriander to flavour his food.

The gorge, he said, had once been inhabited by a fearsome ghoul, who the holy man, after a terrible battle, had chopped to bits with his sword. According to the legend, the ravens had been born from the pieces of the ghoul's body.

I looked at the big black birds on the snow. While we had been talking they had edged closer to the tomb. The man stood up, clapped his hands and shouted. They fluttered up, croaking morosely, before settling again on the snow. A sinister assemblage, they acted like they owned the place.

I noticed a piece of an airplane sticking out of the river. The fellow said it had flown too close to the gorge and had disturbed the ghoul, who had reached up and swatted it like a fly.

During the summer, he said, pilgrims flock from all over Morocco to visit the *koubba*, but I was the first to arrive since the snows began. He offered me several glasses of smoky-tasting tea from his own pot, and half a loaf of home-made bread spread with goat cheese and honey. Nothing could have tasted better.

In the course of our rudimentary exchange, which took a long time because of the language barrier, he referred to a refuge farther up the mountain where I could spend the night. That suited me fine. The sugary tea had refreshed me enormously, so I decided to push on. Taking my soft hand in his rough one, he pointed the way.

Upon reaching the crest of the next ridge, I looked back and there he was, like a character out of a fable, still sitting in front of his *koubba* past which the river plunged so wildly, repairing his boots. I admired the man who accepted his solitude with such calm detachment, who could just go on cheerfully sewing his boots in the sun, and wait for the snow to melt and the next batch of tourists from Casablanca. Seeing him thus, it dawned on me that I had things to learn from Moroccans – important things like accepting fate and how to wait without worrying.

Before setting off I drew a picture of the *koubba* in my notebook. It looks more or less like this:

All afternoon I trudged through powder snow up a long narrow valley. The river, as it sluiced along the ravine below me, had thrown up fantastic ice configurations. Icicles as thick as my leg clung to the cliffs where water trickled in the sun. The snowfields reflected a light that was almost blinding; I was smart to have brought my dark glasses along. Hardly a breath of air stirred. Snow plumes trailing from peaks far above me indicated, however, that strong winds were blowing at higher altitudes. I was glad I wasn't up there. When long blue shadows began to flow down from the ridges, I kept an anxious eye out for the refuge. It would be no joke to be caught out in the snow at an altitude of almost 11,000 feet.

A ray of sun glinted off a tin roof up ahead. The Berber who came out to greet me wasn't dressed in a djellaba. He was wearing instead knickerbockers, knee socks and mountain boots, a quilted parka, wool cap and goggles – all in a very used condition. He wished me a merry Christmas and invited me into the refuge. My blanket reeked of manure, so I left it outside.

His name was Loot and he was an official mountain guide. While relaxing before a pot-bellied stove I noticed a sign on the door which said that the rate was fifty dirhams per night. When I confessed to Loot I only had forty-eight, he laughed away the coins I placed as proof upon the table. After all, he said, it was Christmas. He inquired in a more serious tone if I planned to climb to the top of Jebel Toubkal the following day. When I replied that the idea had never crossed my mind, he seemed puzzled.

Just before dark some other Berbers showed up. Loot prepared a spicy stew which we ate with our fingers and soaked up the sauce with the bread the others had brought. I felt healthy and happy in the company of my new friends. Loot was the only one who spoke any French. Patting my chest, I got it across that I had come up to breathe the excellent mountain air and had never exercised so vigorously in my life. Being mountain men themselves, they applauded my wisdom. They all looked incredibly tough and exuded a gay vitality.

We played a raucous game of blind man's bluff until midnight. For grown men to play a children's game may sound juvenile, but we had a lot of fun. Afterwards we climbed upstairs to a loft. I unrolled my blanket on a mattress next to where the Berbers were sleeping. During the night I could hear them moving away from me one by one, discretely so as not to disturb me, because of the smell.

When I awoke the sun was shining. Downstairs I found Loot brewing a pot of tea. He greeted me in his usual hearty manner and asked if I were ready to tackle the mountain. I looked out the window at a blue wall leading up to a gap between two towering cliffs. It seemed inconceivable that I could scale such a slope, but the idea of even attempting the impossible began to intrigue me. For some reason Loot seemed determined that I should give it a try, and I agreed to have a go. He lent me a pair of boots. Following his instructions, I stuffed the cuffs of my trousers into my socks and wrapped strips of cloth around my legs from ankle to knee, in the form of puttees.

After a breakfast of bread and butter and several glasses of tea, Loot handed me a pair of gloves and some earmuffs, and we set off. Crossing the river on a snow bridge, we attacked the mountain. It wasn't straight up, as it had appeared from the refuge, but the slope was so steep I felt like a fly. Kicking footholds into the frozen snow, Loot led the way. I followed on all fours, like a monkey or a bear. We hadn't climbed for more than a few minutes before I had to sit down and rest. Collapse might be a better word – my lungs were bursting.

In that manner we progressed slowly but steadily – climbing and resting. Loot shouldered a rucksack which contained our lunch. I carried nothing. In his hand he held a slender pole which he used from time to time to test the depth of the snow. After an hour we passed from beneath the cliffs into a wide white basin, where we had a view of the crest with its trailing plume of snow. Loot began to whoop and holler, and I feared his booming peals would loosen the drifts above us. On the contrary, the voice of one small man seemed to dominate the solemn peaks all around. It was inspiring to hear him bellow like that, so I yelled along with him, at the top of my lungs. Together we startled another crowd of croaking ravens, and the impassive mountains returned our voices. It was as though we were the only two men alive, and the world was just beginning, or had recently come to an end.

We mounted the high basin wall, where Loot presented me with an incomparable view from the edge of the mountain. Even the giant eagles swirled far below us. South from the chain of the Atlas, which resembled big scoops of vanilla ice-cream, Loot pointed out the Jebel Sarhro beyond

Ouarzazate, the valleys carved by the rivers Dra and Souss, and the Anti-Atlas Mountains, which form the final barrier to the desert. We could even make out the edge of the Sahara, shimmering and silent, while standing knee-deep in snow.

Although I was worn out, there could be no turning back. Fortified by cheese, bread, and a juicy orange, we made the final ascent. It turned out to be no more difficult than the rest, only a lot scarier. I had to negotiate an icy ridge on my hands and knees while Loot skipped on ahead.

They say the Atlas Mountains have no foothills to speak of, and I can believe it. Standing on the 14,000 foot summit of Jebel Toubkal, surrounded by ice and snow and buffeted by a swirling gale, I was looking down on the hot and dusty plain of Marrakesh, where the red city was faintly visible in the distance. I had to pinch myself: here I was, poised on one of the tallest mountains in Africa, and there, scattered across a lesser peak, lay the wreckage of an airplane that had not flown so high.

From Asni I got a ride back to Marrakesh with a man driving an automobile with tubes of Colgate toothpaste and bars of Palmolive soap painted all over it. He had a long white beard and wore an orange turban and a striped djellaba. He may have only been a travelling salesman, but he spoke with the authority of a priest.

He laughed at the tale of my mountain climbing expedition.

'What are you searching for in my country, my son?' he asked. 'Is it wildness, or is it peace?'

I didn't know, I told him. Maybe both, I said. Maybe they both amount to the same thing.

I think he was glad to get rid of me. The smell of manure from the blanket was so overpowering that we had to drive along with the windows wide open. In the end I gave it to Moktar to cover his horse with.

※

The first thing I did in Marrakesh was cash a travellers cheque. There was a long line of people at the bank, so I had to wait. Just as my turn came, a Moroccan slipped in front of me.

'Makes you have to suppress an urge to kill, doesn't it?' muttered an Englishman standing behind me. He looked disgusted.

'England is famous for its queues, isn't it?' I asked. In London I had admired the way people stood patiently in line, waiting for the bus.

'From now on the only queue that people will respect will be the breadline.'

We ran into each other again on the street and introduced ourselves. His name was Harry Burge. He had come with his mother to Marrakesh on a vacation from Tangier, where he had lived for many years. At first I thought him a rather odd-looking fellow. He was plump and had a red face. Under his nose perched a little brown mustache. His hair was cropped short and, in effect, he had a Germanic appearance. He was about Alice's age.

We had a glass of mint tea together, which made

Harry sweat. Harry was the only Englishman I knew who enjoyed mint tea. He was also the first Englishman I'd met in Morocco who had a job. But then Harry is not really English but Gibraltarian, or Gibraltese. He is a teacher of English at the American Library in Tangier. He also lectures at the Spanish Institute. His mother gives piano lessons when she feels well enough.

'I've been looking for work,' I said, 'but in Tangier there doesn't seem to be anything.'

'What are your qualifications?'

'None, really.'

'You should speak to Miss Toledano. She runs the language school at the American Library. She's always on the lookout for extra teachers. If you can't do anything, you can always teach.'

Besides English, Harry speaks Spanish and French. His mother speaks German. She was once a professor of music at Columbia University. Harry has many fond memories of his stay in New York, although he was only a child at the time.

We agreed to meet again the next day and went for a carriage ride together. We visited the places where I had already been, but I enjoyed the ride much more than before, because Harry was such good company. I volunteered to pay the fare, but Harry insisted on paying half. I didn't think he could really afford it, but then he is very firm about such things.

After that we saw each other regularly. Harry always wore the same light blue checked suit whose trousers barely reached his ankles. One day he put

on a yellow shirt, and the next day a white one –
always clean but never pressed. I think he had only
two shirts and washed them himself. The tie never
varied. It was a wide brown one, which he tied in
such a fat knot that it hung just a few inches down
his chest. On his feet were sandals and socks.

Although we spent part of each day together, I
never saw Harry at night. He had to spend the
evenings with his mother who wasn't feeling well
enough to leave the hotel. I never met Mrs Burge,
but once I talked to her on the telephone when I
called Harry.

'Oh, you're Harry's American friend,' she said,
and we chatted about New York for a few minutes.

'Harry said he's going to try to help me get a job
at the American Library in Tangier,' I said.

There was a moment of silence on the other end
of the line.

'Oh. You shouldn't do that,' she finally said,
'unless you're flat broke.'

Her words surprised me. 'Why not?' I asked.

'You might take some of Harry's hours away from
him. Then I won't even be able to ride the bus.'

She asked me to ring again in an hour. Harry had
gone to the pharmacy and would have returned by
then. After forty-five minutes I called back hoping to
speak to Mrs Burge again. I wanted to assure her that
the last thing I intended was to take Harry's hours,
but I didn't get a chance because Harry answered the
phone. I guess I was disappointed. I don't like
leaving loose ends. Besides, I had enjoyed listening

to the sound of his mother's voice. It was very melodious, and I could believe that she once had a career as a singer.

Harry told me that his mother had been ill for a long time. She had difficulty swallowing and ate very little, mainly soft things like soup and yoghurt. For long periods she was too weak to leave her bed. Then Harry had to do the cooking and marketing and clean the house, besides wait on her. She had to be fed and washed and assisted in going to the toilet.

'I don't really know anything about housekeeping,' he said, wiping his eyes with a handkerchief. Harry suffered from hyperactive tear ducts. 'But someone has to do it. I suppose a man should learn how to cook and iron, for when he gets married he cannot expect his wife to do all the work. I once took cooking lessons. I wanted to learn how to make a soufflé but never got the hang of it. What's more, we cannot afford proper food, and eat meat only twice a week.'

I told him I didn't know anything about cooking, or cleaning, or anything.

'Yes, but I really don't mind it, you know. Except that she seems to be getting worse. I brought her to Marrakesh hoping the change of climate would do her good, but she hasn't been able to leave the hotel room. I don't think there's any hope. I'm afraid she is going to die.'

We fell silent for a moment. I looked at Harry's Spanish briefcase on the table. He never went anywhere without it.

'Is there anything I can do?' I asked.

'No, I don't suppose there's anything anyone can do, but do you ever go over to Gibraltar?'

I told him I went occasionally. Alice and I used to go over to stock up on whiskey and peanut butter, and some dog food for a friend of hers. We had a good time watching English television at the Holiday Inn.

'Well, in that case you might pick up some Jelloids and Milk of Magnesia. You can't get them in Tangier. I can't afford proper medicine, and they do give her some relief.'

I said I would be glad to.

'I shall reimburse you.'

'Of course.'

Harry spoke very well. He expressed his ideas articulately. Although he did most of the talking, he was also interested in whatever I had to say. He is not like some people who grow bored and glassy-eyed the minute the subject changes from themselves.

His two main interests are America and animals. He reads as much about America as he can and keeps in touch with world events on the BBC. The years he spent in New York were the happiest of his life, and he would be there yet if his mother's health hadn't failed and she was forced to leave her teaching position. He knew a lot more about America than I did, and questioned me about the Constitution, the System of Checks and Balances, and States' Rights — subjects I hadn't kept up with. He is a very intelligent person, I thought. A man of culture and inquiry. I admired him.

Harry kept two tortoises in a box.

'They are so sweet,' he said, 'and make such good pets because they don't make noise or bother anyone. Excellent for invalids, ideal for anyone who spends a great deal of time in bed. And very cheap to keep. They eat mostly tomatoes, lettuce, cabbage, and cauliflower. I've had this pair for three years. Before, I had another pair, but I took them to Spain where the climate must have disagreed with them, for they died. One, the male I have now, developed an enormous carbuncle on his neck which I steamed every morning with the kettle until it opened and drained. I was afraid to take him to the vet because he is nervous for a tortoise and might have died from shock. Sensitive creatures, you know. It took two months for the hole to disappear. In the winter I let them out of their box so they can crawl under the electric heater. And their shells are very strong, you know. If I accidentally happen to kick one as it is on its way to the heater or seeking out a place where it can hibernate, it doesn't seem to hurt it at all.'

Harry and his mother had brought the tortoises to Marrakesh, but I never saw them. Every day I used to ask how they were. What with his brown eyes so far apart that they almost seemed to be on the side of his head, and his thick neck which connected his jawbone to his chest without the benefit of a chin, Harry somewhat resembled a tortoise himself. I never told him, of course. He would have been greatly offended. He was very particular about his appearance.

In a short time we became friends. I told him about Alice, my trip to New York, and the visit to the cemetery in Queens.

'There was no headstone, you say?'

'Nothing.'

He thought about it for a while before concurring with the caretaker's explanation. Mayan pyramids, he said, have been toppled when the earth moves.

'The man at the gate – did he act suspiciously in any way?'

I recalled he was a friendly fellow who seemed to enjoy his work.

'And the sister – what about her?'

'Lois. Well, I know for a fact that she never liked the idea of our travelling together.'

'A jealous one, perhaps. Married?'

'She was married. Divorced now.'

'A jealous one to be sure. Jealous of her sister. Not uncommon, that.'

'She sounded angry that I'd slept late and missed the funeral.'

'And she spread it all over New York, you say?'

This particular detail fascinated Harry. He seemed to think that missing the funeral had made me into some kind of celebrity, as though the event had been announced over the radio.

'Everyone I spoke to had heard about it. I could tell from the sound of their voices, whether they mentioned it or not.'

'That's female vindictiveness for you.' Harry shook his head sadly. 'I don't know how many empires it's brought down. No, I am sure she must be dead.'

'I guess you're right.'

We didn't say anything for a while. I still become sad when I think of Alice under the ground in Queens. She was the sporty type and loved fresh air. That was one of the reasons she left New York. Never got enough of it there, she used to say.

'However, I have read about cases of people being buried alive by mistake,' Harry continued. 'They were thought to be dead when they were only in a temporary, death-like coma.'

'How was anybody able to tell afterwards whether they were dead or alive?'

'For some reason or another the bodies were dug up. By grave robbers, I suppose, looking for human hair. It continues to grow, you know, long after the body is dead, and used to have quite a good value before they could duplicate it artificially. Apparently the inside of the coffin lids were found to be scratched where the person tried to claw his way out. The fingertips were worn down to the bone . . .'

We were quiet again.

'But even so,' I said, 'Alice would surely be dead by now. After all, it's been over a month.'

'Yes. Of course. I hadn't thought of that.'

※

A few days later Harry took his mother back to Tangier. She wasn't feeling any better and wanted to go home. I gave him my telephone number. He promised to call. I left shortly afterwards myself. My breathing had improved but, after having such good company as Harry, it wasn't much fun being in Marrakesh on my own.

One of the first things I did was to take the ferry over to Gibraltar to buy some Jelloids and Milk of Magnesia. Gibraltar wasn't the same without Alice. It's a dirty little town where they don't seem to speak either English or Spanish, but a combination of the two that's not easy to understand. I was glad to get back to Tangier.

Naturally, I expected Harry to call. I stayed near the phone, but it never rang. His name wasn't in the phone book and, as he hadn't given me his address, I had no way of contacting him. He said he and his mother lived in an apartment, not a proper apartment but a converted office in a deserted office building that had been under construction when Tangier's building boom had abruptly come to an end. Harry said that rusty iron bars stuck out of the roof. Apparently it was an unhealthy place to live because of the damp. All the other occupants had moved out. The paint was peeling off the walls, and the plaster kept coming loose from the ceiling and falling on them. The landlord never made any repairs. According to Harry, he was a lazy Spaniard from Andalucia with shiny yellow skin and a pencil mustache. He never failed, however, to appear at their door on the first day of each month to collect the rent. Even the doctor resisted paying calls on them in such a place, for fear of catching cold. Harry admitted that sometimes it was like living in a cave. But they didn't have the money to rent a proper apartment, and had been there such a long time that they had grown used to the inconveniences.

Mohamed and I cruised the back streets of Tangier looking for a building that matched Harry's description, but we never found it. The more I saw of Tangier, the more I realized that a lot of buildings fitted into this category. Laundry hung out of the windows, and gangs of children ruled the streets. In some neighbourhoods Mohamed rolled up the windows and wouldn't let me get out of the car.

My money, meanwhile, was running low. The joint account that Alice had opened at the bank dried up, so I was forced to close it. I got into the habit of taking my travellers cheques out each night and counting them. The rent on the house, reasonable as it was, began to feel more and more expensive. If I was going to go on living in Tangier, I'd either have to find a job, sell the car, or both. So I decided to go down to the American Library and try my luck there.

The American Library is a three-cornered building located at a busy intersection where the Arab and European quarters meet. It sticks out into the street like the bow of a ship. I walked in, and there was Harry, sitting at one of the tables, reading a magazine. I took a copy of *Time* from the shelf and sat down next to him.

'Hello, Harry,' I said.

He looked up from his magazine. 'Oh, hello, Norman. How are you?'

I said I was fine and asked why he hadn't called.

'My mother died.'

At first I couldn't think of what to say. I noticed he was wearing a black arm band. Maybe I should have gotten one, too, because of Alice, but it was a little late.

'When did it happen?' I asked.

'A week ago tomorrow.'

'Did you go to the funeral?'

'Yes, of course I did. Why shouldn't I have?'

'I don't know. I just asked,' I said, thinking it was a dumb question.

'It was the next day. I couldn't afford a proper funeral, you know, with flowers and all the trim-mings, so I just had her buried.'

'I'm really sorry, Harry.'

'About what?'

'That your mother died.'

'Oh.'

'How did it happen?'

'I'm not sure. I wasn't there.'

'Where were you?'

'Downstairs.'

While we were talking, a woman dressed in black entered the Library. As soon as she saw Harry, she changed direction and hurried over to our table. She walked with a limp.

'Oh, Harry,' she said.

Harry looked up. 'Hello, Miss Toledano.'

'I've just got back from Madrid, Harry. I heard about your mother this morning, in the market. I'm so sorry.'

'Thank you.'

She sat down at the table. 'How did it happen?' she asked.

Harry took out a handkerchief and wiped his eyes.

'Well, you see, she had taken a turn for the worse after we came back from Marrakesh. Now I realize that it was a mistake to have gone there. After all the rain we had here in Tangier, I thought the sunshine would lift her spirits, but the dust got into her throat, and she never did recover her strength from that gruelling bus trip. I telephoned Dr Gomez. I could tell from the sound of his voice that he didn't like the idea much, but he promised to come at eight o'clock.'

'You know he's not a proper doctor, Harry,' Miss Toledano said, glancing at me. 'He studied medicine in Madrid for a few years but never took his exams.'

'We have him because he doesn't charge us, as he used to be one of my pupils. Well, at seven-thirty I went downstairs to wait. They lock the door to our building early. By eight-thirty he hadn't arrived. I knew he wasn't coming, but I just kept on waiting. I didn't want to go up and tell my mother that he hadn't come. She never complains, but I just didn't want to disappoint her.'

Harry's hand was moving aimlessly around the table. Miss Toledano covered it with her own and held it until it stopped trembling.

'So I just sat there on the steps,' he went on, 'and watched the cars go by. It was a warm night, it had just rained, and I must have dozed off. The noise of passing cars can be quite soporific, you know, especially when the pavement is wet.'

Miss Toledano glanced at me and smiled.

'When I looked at my watch again, it was nine o'clock. I went upstairs. The light was still burning in my mother's room, but she didn't say anything when I entered the flat. Usually she calls out, "Is that you, Harry?" As if it could be anyone else. I thought she was asleep. I was about to go into her room to turn off the light in order to save on the electricity, but, as she is such a light sleeper, I refrained, for fear of waking her. The next morning I discovered that she had not been sleeping at all, but was dead instead. She was already cold and stiff, like a kitten I had once that died.'

We were quiet for a minute. I looked at Miss Toledano's hands on the table, where they covered Harry's. Two of her fingers were wrapped with Band-Aids. Her fingernails were painted a fiery red. The skin around her nails was badly gnawed. She wore no rings.

'I'll miss her piano concerts at the Goethe Institute,' she said.

Harry nodded.

'She had so much talent.'

'Wasted in Tangier.'

'She also had a beautiful voice,' I added.

Miss Toledano looked at me again. Her eyes were

dark brown and almond-shaped. She had strong
eyebrows, and her skin was a kind of lemony brown.
Except for her black clothes, which looked Spanish
or South American, she could have passed for a
Moroccan.

'That's right, she did,' she said.

'I didn't actually know her,' I said. 'I just spoke to
her over the phone.'

'She was quite a personality, wasn't she, Harry?'

Harry wiped his eyes.

'Do you remember the time after that recital she
gave at the Italian School she wouldn't get into the
taxi I had ordered, even though it was beginning to
rain?'

'We walked all the way home and got soaking
wet,' Harry said.

Miss Toledano shot me another bright smile. 'Mrs
Burge didn't want to share her man, not even for ten
minutes.'

Harry blushed when she said that.

'Where is she buried, Harry? I'd like to take some
flowers to her grave.'

'At the International Cemetery. I couldn't get her
into the English Cemetery.'

'Why not?'

'That's where she wanted to be, but I was rebuffed
by the vicar.'

'What do you mean?'

'He said there wasn't any room.'

'Of course, there's room!' Miss Toledano's eyebrows contracted to project a fierce look.

'Not for my mother. He said all the plots have been reserved. By English society people, I suppose, who organize benefits for the church. We never belonged to that set. Besides, I didn't have the money to pay for a proper funeral.'

'That's terrible, Harry!'

'Oh, Miss Toledano, people are so indifferent!' Harry blew his nose and wiped his eyes. This time it wasn't his tear ducts acting up. We waited for a few minutes for the sobs to subside.

'I'm sorry,' he gasped.

'You must keep busy, Harry, keep teaching,' she said firmly, giving his hand a squeeze. 'Will you let me know if there's anything I can do?'

Harry's eyes were down. He nodded dejectedly.

'Are you getting enough to eat?'

He nodded again.

'Would you like me to bring you some soup?'

'I like your chicken soup.'

'All right.'

✳

'Is that the Miss Toledano you were telling me about in Marrakesh?' I asked Harry after she went away.

'Yes. She runs the language school.'

'She's very beautiful.'

'She's beautiful, she comes from a big family, but she's alone.'

'Why is that?'

'Everyone in Tangier is alone,' he said, wiping away the tears.

We were silent for a minute. Harry picked up his

Scientific American and started making notes on a scrap of paper. I glanced at *Time*. There was no point in telling Harry that I had gone over to Gibraltar and bought some Jelloids and Milk of Magnesia, now that his mother was dead.

'Harry,' I said. 'I have an idea.'

'What is it?'

'How would you like to come up and live in my house?'

He thought about it for a minute. 'I think I better stay where I am.'

'I have the car. Mohamed could drive you into town any time you wanted.'

'I don't think so.'

'Fatima will cook the food you like.'

He shook his head.

'I bet your tortoises would like my garden, Harry.'

'No, Norman, not now.'

Naturally, I was disappointed. Having Harry in the house would have meant two fewer lonely people living in Tangier. We could have taken rides in the car and stayed up late talking. Fatima and I were running out of conversation. More often than not we just sipped mint tea in the kitchen while she corrected my Arabic. What's more, I was getting a little tired of mint tea. But I understood how Harry felt. I wouldn't want to move out of my house, either.

'What are you going to do with your mother's clothes, Harry?'

'What?' He seemed surprised by my question.

'I have a closet full of clothes that belonged to Alice.'

'I suppose you can give them to the Adoratrices. The nuns.'

'What do the nuns do with them?'

'I think they distribute them to the poor.'

✳

After Harry left I went over to Miss Toledano's desk. She was chatting away in Spanish over the phone. The desk was stacked with books. Peeking out from between the piles was a pre-Columbian *huaco*, like the ones I had brought back from Peru. Hers was in the shape of a spotted sitting cat – a jaguar. While waiting for her to finish I thought I noticed a kind of fishy smell in the air.

'Are you a friend of Harry?' she asked when she hung up.

'I've only known him for a week, but yes, I am.'

'We're going to have to take care of him now.'

'All right.'

'He lived alone with his mother. There isn't any-one else.'

'I know.'

'How often do you see him?'

'Today is the first time since Marrakesh. But that's because I didn't know where he lived.'

'It's important that he has people to talk to, especially over the next few weeks.'

'In Marrakesh we saw each other every day.'

'Good. If we work together he won't be left alone.'

The telephone rang, and I had to wait again. This time she spoke in French. I liked the way she dressed. Her black clothes gave her a stylish, formal look that you wouldn't normally expect in a librarian, or maybe in what I would imagine a chic Parisian librarian to be.

'Harry said I should ask you if there was a job open teaching English,' I said when she had finished.

She leaned back in her chair. She wore a silk blouse with a deep floppy collar that exposed an alluring wink of cleavage. Her lips were painted a deep red. The colour contrasted strongly with the severity her clothes. Her hair was covered by a black turban, not the Moroccan kind that you wrap, but one which fits over the head like a fashionable hat. I guessed she was about thirty years old. Maybe thirty-five.

'Do you have any experience teaching English?' she asked.

I was about to mention Harry's remark about people who don't know how to do anything can always teach, but decided against it.

'I'm afraid not.'

She asked if I had a college degree. I told her I had to quit after my sophomore year. The pressure of exams nearly always triggered an attack. I was planning a career in architecture, but it didn't work out.

'I guess my only qualification for teaching English is that I speak English,' I said.

She handed me a form to fill out. While I was

writing, the telephone rang again. This time she rattled away in Arabic.

After she hung up she asked where I came from. New York, I said, more or less. She said that's where she grew up, too.

'Where did you learn all those languages?' I asked.

'Oh, my mother used to take me travelling all over the place,' she answered evasively.

'You're lucky.' I handed back the paper. 'The closest I ever got to a foreign language in America was high school Spanish.'

I asked her about the *huaco*. She said she had lived in Cuzco for two years working for UNESCO and had got it there.

'I've been to Cuzco,' I said.

Her dark eyebrows contracted into a scowl.

'Everybody said to watch out for *siroche*,' I went on. 'You know, mountain sickness. But the thin Andean air didn't bother me at all. In fact I breathed very well there. Maybe that's because I have this enlarged chest,' I said, patting it. 'Like the Indians who live at those high altitudes.'

'Why is that?' The scowl vanished when she smiled. 'Why do you have an enlarged chest?'

'Asthma. Chronic coughing stretches the lungs, you know. What made me nervous in Cuzco were the earth tremors. A big one shook the city when I was there. It threw me out of bed at five in the morning. I woke up on the floor, still reeling from a vivid dream that I have never forgotten. The light bulb dangling from the ceiling was swinging back and forth.'

The fierce look suddenly returned to Miss Toledano's face. She began to sniff the air like an animal.

'Do you smell something funny?' she asked.

'I wasn't going to say so, but yes, I do,' I said. 'I smell fish.'

Glancing at the books on her desk, she pulled a pile toward her and started going through them. She let out a shriek when she came to one with a fish head sticking out. Everyone in the library looked up. Opening the book, she lifted out a sardine skeleton by its tail.

'What's that doing there?' I asked.

'It's a bookmark!' she said, pinching her nose shut.

'A dead fish?'

She started laughing.

'Who puts dead fish inside books?'

'My uncle, Moyses Bendahan. He runs the Bazar Franco-Inglés down the street.'

'And he puts dead fish inside books.'

'The kindest old man you can imagine, but totally absent-minded! We call him Papa Noël because of his long white beard. The last time he was reading a book during his lunch break, a customer came into his shop.' She folded the skeleton inside a sheet of newspaper and dropped the bundle into the waste-basket. 'He absent-mindedly placed a half-eaten sardine on the page as a kind of bookmark, shut the book and forgot all about it. Now he's done it again!'

'Well, he picked the skeleton clean, like a cat would do. Otherwise it would smell even worse.'

Miss Toledano had a loud, explosive laugh that reminded me a little of Alice's. Everybody in the library was smiling.

A group of students approached her desk with some questions, so we had to cut our conversation short.

'I just remembered,' I said getting to my feet. 'When I was in Peru, I taught English to a Peruvian family to earn some extra cash. Only for a week, if that counts as experience.'

I said goodbye and walked out of the American Library feeling happy for three reasons. I was back in touch with Harry. I had finally filled out a job application. And three, Miss Toledano and I had things in common – Harry. And Peru.

✳

Although he stayed on in his apartment, Harry and I saw each other regularly. He enjoyed riding in my car. Otherwise he had to walk, for he couldn't afford taxis, and in Tangier the bus service is unreliable.

One day I mixed up a thermos full of martinis and told Mohamed to take us in the direction of Tetuan. But Harry didn't want a martini.

'My mother and I were teetotallers,' he said.

I drank one martini and poured the rest out the window. But we had a good time anyhow. Harry liked to talk and I enjoyed listening to him. He talked mostly about his mother and the life they led.

89

They had spent almost all their time together attending concerts, lectures and other cultural events that I didn't realize were part of life for Europeans residing in Tangier.

'We were never included in any circle of English friends,' he said. 'Most of the English in Tangier bring their habits with them and do the same kind of things they did back in England.'

'Like drinking tea with lemon or milk?'

'That sort of thing. They go to bars and give parties, play cards and gossip. My mother and I were never much interested in that.'

I didn't tell Harry that Alice and I used to go the bars quite a lot ourselves.

'I miss having her in the flat. Even if we didn't say a word to each other all day long, I always knew she was there.'

I told him I understood how he felt.

'I'm too old to be alone or free.'

Every day Harry went to the cemetery to lay fresh flowers by his mother's grave. I waited outside the gate in the car until he came out, hot and sweating from being in the sun, his breasts bobbing up and down beneath a new nylon shirt he had just bought. Once I asked him if he minded if I accompanied him to the graveside, but he said he preferred to be alone, which I could understand. I thought of going one day by myself but, as Harry might not have approved, I didn't.

Another project he occupied himself with was the preparation of his mother's tombstone. We called on an Italian who traded in marble. The white stone Harry wanted was unavailable, so he had to choose another. It came from Portugal and was pink with green lines running through it. The appropriate words were being inscribed.

✳

One day the telephone rang. It was Miss Toledano. One of her teachers had dropped out, and there was a place for me. On a trial basis, of course, and only three days a week, but I jumped at it. The pay wasn't much, but it gave me something to do.

'I won't be taking any of Harry's hours away from him, will I?'

'He takes the advanced courses. You'll be teaching the beginners.'

Mohamed drove me in the car. Just four students came to my class, young Moroccans from poor families who hoped that learning English would improve their chances of finding jobs in Tangier. I told them I hoped they were right. Mostly we conversed in English, or they read aloud. I parsed some sentences for them on the blackboard. I like parsing sentences. It's one of the things I'm good at.

Miss Toledano sat in on my class to see how I was doing. She said I was doing fine, but noticed that the students seemed bewildered by the big diagrams I drew on the blackboard. It was not a realistic exercise for keeping the class's attention, she said, so I stopped doing that.

Although Miss Toledano scowled when she talked, it didn't mean she was angry. It was just a habit she had of knitting her eyebrows when she was concentrating. Probably she's a little far-sighted, I thought, like those owls in a cage that blink when bringing you into focus.

In spite of her handicap, she went everywhere on foot. Her purse she carried inside a Moroccan straw basket with a leather strap. She never put on a hat or a coat, even when it was cold. Sometimes I'd see her from the car, a solitary figure in black limping determinedly to work among the Moroccans in their flowing robes and floppy straw hats. Her handicap caused her to walk sideways; her shoulders were not always square to the direction in which she was heading. This may sound strange, but the sight of her hobbling along in that crowd of strangers made me want to take her hand and walk beside her down a long, lonely road.

I even had a dream about her.

One wet day I asked Mohamed to stop the car and offered her a lift. She climbed in and sat beside me in the back, like Alice used to do. The strong perfume she wore came in with her.

'Guess what I found in the market today,' she said excitedly.

'What?'

She reached into her basket and lifted out a clear plastic sack half filled with water. Thousands of tiny white worms were swimming around inside.

'*Hay angulas!*' She almost shouted the words.

'Ugh! What are they?'

'Baby eels, or elvers. They grow up in the rivers

of Morocco and swim all the way to the Sargasso Sea
to spawn. These little ones spend three years floating
back across the Atlantic on currents before finding
the river their parents left. No one knows how they
do it. It's one of nature's mysteries that science can't
explain. You catch them during the rainy season, but
it's almost impossible to get them anymore because
the fishing is controlled by the authorities who send
them to Madrid where they command a fantastic
price. A fisherman came up to me in the market this
morning and said he netted them at night when the
police were asleep.'

I looked closer. Each transparent eel was about an
inch or two long. You could see their stomachs
inside.

'What are you going to do with them?'

'I'm going to eat them!'

'*Angulas – muy ricas*,' Mohamed commented ap-
provingly from the front seat.

'Would you like some?' she asked.

'Well, I'll try anything once.'

'Bravo! I'll cook them for you at my place!'

Miss Toledano's enthusiasm was contagious. All
of a sudden it was like life was starting up all over
again

'How would you like me to pick you up at your
place on the days I go to the Library?' I
volunteered.

'I prefer to walk, Norman.'

'That shopping basket looks pretty heavy.'

'It's the only exercise I ever get.'

'What about on rainy days?'

'Thank you, Norman. I do have a car. That reminds me – I need to go to the automobile club and get my international driving licence.'

I couldn't help feeling disappointed. It was cosy having Miss Toledano with me in the car. She wore a combination of powerful Moroccan perfumes – orange blossom oil for fragrance, she said, and essence of camomile to calm her down. The scent lingered in the car after she got out.

As the American Library kept Spanish hours, with a two hour lunch break, I invited Harry and Miss Toledano to a restaurant on the beach, a place where Alice and I used to go. The summer season hadn't started yet, so there weren't any tourists. The Moroccan waiter greeted me like an old friend. It had been a long winter, business was slow, and he was glad to have some customers again. As the temperature of the air was warmer outside than in, he volunteered to carry a table from the restaurant and set it up on the sand, so we could sit in the sun. A soccer game ebbed and flowed across the wide beach. The shouts of the young players struggling for the ball drifted on the wind. Hungry seagulls wheeled above our heads.

We ordered grilled sardines, Moroccan salad and a bottle of wine. I liked watching Miss Toledano eat. She ate with little slurps and trills of delight. I never saw anyone enjoy food so much, but somehow she managed to stay slim. She showed me how to eat a grilled sardine. Picking up the fish with her fingers, she held it at each end, like you do with corn on the cob. The trick is to bend the fish toward you so the flesh breaks off in boneless flecks.

The alley cats crouching by the wall wolfed the skeletons we threw their way. Feeling a little drunk, I tossed breadcrusts at the seagulls. Miss Toledano clapped her hands when they caught them in mid-air.

After lunch she went into one of the bathhouses to change. I shut myself in another. From where I was standing I could see her bare feet on the sand beneath the cubicle door. She lifted one foot then the other as she stepped out of her clothes. The door opened, and she came out wearing a black terrycloth bikini. Her arms and legs were slim, and the fuzzy terrycloth lifted her breasts, which were already quite large. One of her knees was criss-crossed by a number of livid scars. They etched a painful patchwork on her lemony-brown skin.

Harry did not want to swim. He stayed at the table talking to the waiter while Miss Toledano and I walked down to the water. She had difficulty crossing the beach. Her leg, the one with the scars, was stiff. She couldn't seem to bend her knee.

When we reached the edge of the water, we dropped our towels and waded out through the waves.

'Swimming is my favourite sport,' I said while we were treading water. 'It's about the only form of exercise I can take without getting winded.'

'I love the water,' she said.

'I don't swim very well, but when I was younger I wanted to be a life-guard. Unfortunately I never had the endurance for training.'

'I love the water,' she repeated, a bit ruefully, 'because it gets me off my feet.'

'I never take a bath in summer,' I said. 'I just go to the beach and shower when I get home to wash off the salt.'

'Once a week I go to the hammam with a Moroccan friend. The public baths – they're one of Islam's great institutions. We stay for hours and feel wonderfully clean, not only outside but inside, too. After spending a long time purifying your body, you feel a kind of inner peace. You should try it, Norman. There are hours for men, and hours for women.'

We swam side by side. Unlike her movements on land, Miss Toledano was a graceful swimmer. She kept her head out of the water and never took off her turban.

'One time I saved a woman from drowning,' I said when we got back to the beach.

'I thought you said you weren't a strong swimmer.'

'It happened sort of by accident.' Handing her a towel I couldn't helping admiring her body. Her brown skin was wet and sleek, like seal's. 'Do you remember the Peruvian family I told you about? The one I gave English lessons to? One Sunday they invited me to a picnic on the beach outside Lima.'

'Was it Herradura Beach?'

'That's the one. The tide was out, and the beach

looked half a mile wide, with the big Pacific surf thundering in the distance. The sand was so hot you could hardly walk on it. The mother of the family served us fried chicken and went off for a swim by herself. I was sitting under the umbrella with her husband and children when I saw her waving from the ocean. We all saw her, far away because the beach was so wide, and we all waved back. Nobody paid much attention, we were all busy eating lunch, but I thought I noticed something odd about the way she waved, like she was trying to tell us something. Still chewing on a piece of fried chicken, I got up and walked down toward the water. Pretty soon I broke into a trot because the sand was so hot. Maybe it was that trot that saved her, because if I had arrived a minute afterwards, it might have been too late.'

'Norman, you're giving me goose pimples!'

'The closer I got to the water, the more certain I became that something was wrong. Those big Pacific breakers were rolling over her. She kept disappearing under the water, resurfacing, and waving. Then another comber buried her. It wasn't the happy wave of a woman enjoying herself in the ocean, but a frantic signal of distress.'

'That beach is so dangerous! People drown there every year!'

'The minute I entered the surf, I understood what the problem was. A powerful river of cold water was pulling at my legs. I was only standing knee-deep, but it was all I could do to keep my balance. I waded out through the waves, almost up to my shoulders, until I got hold of her hand. She was exhausted from fighting the current and had no strength left. It was a struggle to get her back to the beach. The waves kept crushing us. She could hardly stand up and rested in the shallow water for a few minutes before we rejoined the picnic.'

'Didn't anyone see you? Didn't they come to help?'

'No one said anything about it. I led her back to her family, but maybe she was too tired to talk. I don't think the children had any idea their mother was in difficulty. Her husband was taking a nap.'

'Norman, if it weren't for you she might have drowned right there in front of their eyes!'

'I didn't think anything more about it until about a year later, when I was back in New York. I received a letter from the woman's elder son. He apologized for not writing sooner, but he didn't have my address. He said that every day for the past year his mother had gone to church to light a candle and say a prayer for me. He wanted to express his gratitude, from him and his entire family, for saving his mother's life.'

'You risked your life to save her. Doesn't that make you proud?'

'It still gives me a warm feeling to know that she was praying for me every day, watching over me like a guardian angel without my being aware of it.'

We walked back toward the restaurant. Once more Miss Toledano had difficulty in the soft sand. I offered her my arm. She gripped it with both hands and held on tight.

'Tell me about your dream,' she said, a little out of breath.

'What dream?' For a second I thought she had somehow guessed that I had been dreaming about her.

'The one you had in Cuzco when the earthquake hit.'

'In my dream the central heating system in our house was being torn down. There was a terrific hammering from above, and a rain of ashes, dust, and rust. All this was happening in my room at home. There were no books anywhere, only some old dog beds I was trying to save. I remember my panic mingled with a sense of relief. The system was old, rusty and dirty, and needed to be replaced. I woke up with my heart pounding. Not from the earthquake but from the dream. I could hear it squeaking between my ears, like my little sister jumping up and down on the bed.'

'What do you think it means?'

'I suppose it was a kind of aftershock from my parents' divorce. You know, the warmth of our family home being dismantled. I don't like to talk about these things in front of Harry,' I added, 'since he's missing his mother enough already.'

'But you must talk about it, Norman,' she insisted. I promised I would.

'The only way to dispel sadness is to talk about it.'

'Normally, I would consider family matters to be of minor interest to others.'

'There is no minor and no major,' she whispered, giving my arm a squeeze.

Miss Toledano's hobby was cooking. On another sunny day she packed a picnic lunch, and Mohamed dropped the three of us off at a little cove at the bottom of the Old Mountain where a stream empties into the sea. The Moroccan name for the cove is Merkala. The view from California, one of Tangier's hilly suburbs, has prompted foreign residents to christen the cove 'the champagne cup.' Two gently converging hills form the sides of the cup, and the sea view beyond, with the sunlight glinting off the water, gives the impression that the cup is filled with a clear, sparking liquid.

Miss Toledano spread a blanket in a pasture overlooking the sea where some sheep were grazing. The shepherd was visible on a hummock of ground some way off. She had prepared several dishes: black olives and spicy green olives, chicken liver paté with pickles, a cold bean dish with specks of chorizo, a bottle of wine, and a loaf of French bread.

After lunch Miss Toledano and I walked down to the beach. Harry stayed behind to guard the picnic from the sheep. With no wind, the Strait of Gibraltar was like a mirror. Distant fishing boats dotted the sea like flies on a window pane. We were in Africa, but we could make out the white villages of Andalucia across the water. We felt we could almost reach out and touch the Pillars of Hercules. Moroccan fisher-men stood like statues on the rocks, dowsing the sea with their long bamboo poles.

'Alice loved this view,' I said. 'It's one of the reasons we rented our house.'

'Good, Norman, good.'

The sea looked enticing, but we had forgotten to bring our bathing suits.

'I suppose we could swim in our underwear,' I ventured.

'I would if it were just us, and if I were wearing black underwear,' she laughed, 'but with what I've got on, it would be like swimming stark naked in front of all these fishermen!'

We took off our shoes. Miss Toledano hiked up her skirt, knotting it about her hips. The scars on her knee gleamed like ivory against her brown skin. We waded into the shallow water.

The tide was out, and we walked onto a shelf of rocks to inspect the tidal pools. The rocks were slippery, and she held my arm to steady herself. She didn't have good balance, but her grip was strong, and her fingernails dug into my arm.

The pools had produced crops of seaweed that looked like bright green lettuce. We peered at the colonies of sea urchins, mussels clinging to the rock, the shy fish and lurking crabs. I guided her hand to a colourful sea anemone. She cried out when the creature clung to her finger with its sticky tentacles.

We sat down side by side on a rock. From a pocket in her skirt Miss Toledano produced a silver cigarette case. She flicked it open. Inside two hand-rolled cigarettes lay side by side.

'What's that?' I asked.

'Kif mixed with tobacco,' she said, offering the case. 'Want one?'

'No thanks.'

She took one of the cigarettes from the case, placed it between her lips, and snapped the case shut. A lighter flared. Sitting on the rock, she carried the cigarette to her mouth with her right hand, the left resting on her knee, and inhaled deeply.

From where we sat we could see Harry in the pasture. The shepherd boy had joined him. The notes of a flute wafted on the breeze.

'Harry says you come from a big family,' I said.

'There are only a few of us left.' The words came out with the smoke. 'And if I don't do something about it, soon there won't be anyone.'

'What do you mean?'

She smoked for a minute before answering.

She lived with her two brothers, she said, both of whom were stricken with muscular dystrophy. As children they had walked too long on their tiptoes. When the doctor examined them, he explained to her father, who had been encouraging them to walk properly, that his method was incorrect. Neither boy ever walked again. And now her sister in Boston had just made it known that her young son was showing the same disturbing symptoms. Miss Toledano was worried that she too might be a carrier and transmit the disease to her child, should she have one.

Women carry the disease, she told me, but only males come down with it. Her household was plagued by the curse and the resulting guilt. She had to cut short her stay in Peru to come to Tangier to look after her brothers.

'The house was a mess because only men were living there. The first thing I noticed, even before I walked in the front door, was that the garden sprinkler was broken. I fixed it. It broke again. I fixed it again. After that I compulsively tried to fix everything that had been neglected for years. I weeded the drive and raked it. I mended the kitchen sink, stopped the toilets from running, and put a new lock on the front door. The wiring was so rotten, I got a shock every time I plugged in the hairdryer. I ended up having the whole house rewired. I long to have an electric drill. I've always had to borrow, but I'm a whiz at using it'

I told her I liked doing repairs around the house, too.

'I'm so glad! All those cozy things clustered around your flat, including the Moroccan grocer you can go to in your dressing gown. Very important, that.'

Tangier was her refuge, her 'nest away from the world,' as she called it, but Peru was the love of her life, and she dreamed about going back. Any day now she was expecting another offer from UNESCO to work in Cuzco. She and a Peruvian friend had made plans to open a restaurant in the Andes. It was located above the snowline and would be open only three months a year.

Now, at thirty-two, she dreamed about the joy of producing a baby. On the way to Peru she planned to stop in New York for a series of complicated tests which would determine whether she was a carrier or not. But she was worried about who would take care of her brothers while she was gone. Both were confined to wheelchairs. They were becoming more difficult and demanding. They refused the special diets the doctor had recommended.

'What is it about Peru that keeps you going back?' I asked.

'I feel free there, even though I don't have one minute to myself.'

'Why is that?'

'Because there's so much to do. The people are demoralized after the revolution. The country schools were destroyed by the terrorists. The teachers who weren't murdered ran away.'

'It sounds dangerous.'

'The political situation is more stable now, but the rural educational system has to rebuilt. Books have to be redistributed. There are so many ways I can help. They need me there.'

'More than you brothers need you?'

She tugged on the cigarette. 'To fly, wings need to be exercised. Passion produces passion. Need produces need. They don't need me as much as I thought they did. I want to have a baby one day.' She blew out the smoke. 'I want to move out!'

'Do you plan to get married first?' I asked.

Her eyebrows contracted, and she gave me a

challenging look when I said that.

'Have a smoke,' she said, offering the cigarette. 'You won't get hooked on one puff.'

'No thanks. When I get married, it'll be forever.'

'How do you know that?'

'Because I'll never get a divorce. I've already been through one divorce in my life – my parents' – and once is enough.'

We were quiet for a few minutes.

'I could stay here all afternoon' She sighed and leaned her head against my shoulder.

'I know another big pool further on.'

'No,' she said firmly, rubbing out the cigarette out on the rock. 'It's not fair to leave Harry alone for too long.'

✳

Every Sunday evening Harry and I ate supper together in a little French restaurant on the boulevard. He always insisted on paying his share, saying he was a little richer now that he didn't have to spend so much on medicine.

I asked him to tell me about Miss Toledano.

'You're in love with her, aren't you!' he suddenly blurted out.

'No, I'm not.'

'You are! I can tell. Have you kissed her?'

'Only in a dream I had about her.'

'Well, you can't have her! She belongs to someone else.'

'Who?'

Harry didn't say anything for a while. The other

people in the restaurant had stopped eating. That's Tangier for you. The diners at the next table may be chattering away in Arabic or Italian, but they understand many languages.

'Why does she wear black?' I asked.

'She always dresses that way.'

'Is she in mourning for somebody?'

'I don't think so.'

'What happened to her leg?'

'As a child she had tuberculosis in the knee. Her mother took her to surgeons in Paris and Zurich, but they made a hash of it. As a result of so much surgery, her knee is frozen. That's why she can't bend it.'

'Why is she in Tangier?'

'She was born here.'

'I thought she was American.'

'She has an American passport, but she was born in Morocco.'

'So that's why she speaks so many languages.'

'She comes from an old Jewish family who fled Spain centuries ago to escape the Inquisition,' Harry said. 'They settled in Tangier and became prosperous in the tea and sugar trade here. She still has the key to their house in Granada, and she speaks Ladino.'

'What's that?'

'A medieval Spanish dialect that is still spoken in places where the Sephardim escaped to – Morocco, the Balkans, and some places in South America.'

'She poured out her family problems to me, she

told me about her brothers, but I guess there are still big gaps.'

Harry nodded. 'When the Arab-Israeli troubles began, most of the Jews left Morocco. The poor ones went to Israel, and rich families like the Toledanos emigrated to America. Then a few years ago the Sultan of Morocco, hoping to give a lift to the economy, invited the Jews back. And Miss Toledano's brothers did come back. God knows why – being invalids and with so much hostility against the Jews in the Arab world. One reason is that the family still owns property here – a big square merchant's house on the Marshan, the kind you see occupying prominent positions in Mediterranean ports from Tangier to Thessalonica – where she lives with her brothers. Both are educated, both have law degrees from New York University, but neither has a job.'

'That's why she came to Tangier, she said – to look after them.'

Harry frowned. 'There's another reason.'

'What is it?'

'Don Carlos Bermudez.'

'Who's that?'

'A tall, distinguished Castillian aristocrat she met when she was living in Madrid. At least twenty years older than her. He's the Spanish Consul General here in Tangier. After two years in South America, Madrid seemed tame. She loves Tangier, but she resisted the idea of returning here permanently, knowing that it would be to a life of drudgery, looking after her brothers. But when Don Carlos was posted to Tangier, he begged her to join him, and she accepted. He calls her "Africa."'

'Why?'

'After *la Virgen de Africa*. It's a common name for Spanish girls born in Morocco, and I suppose it seemed appropriate for someone who felt at home the minute she set foot back on the North African shore.'

'Do you think they're lovers?'

'That's what everyone says.'

My heart sank when Harry said that.

✻

Fatima's *sobrina* was suffering from a skin disease which the doctors in Tangier were unable to cure. As a last resort she wanted to take the girl to a sacred spring near Fez, whose water was famous for its restorative powers. As Mohamed volunteered to drive them, I lent him the car for a few days.

So I had to ride the bus, one of the sky blue Volvos recently imported by the Tangier bus company to replace its fleet of ageing brown and yellow Renaults.

Like a block of ice chipped from a Scandinavian glacier, the bus was inching along, pushing ahead of it a moraine of shoppers through Dradeb, one of Tangier's poorest *barrios* – also known to foreign residents as 'Suicide Village,' because so many automobile accidents happen there. Beneath the fierce North African sun, the bus's cool blue hue had already begun to fade. Overcrowding, the dents from countless accidents, and shoddy maintenance had taken their toll. The bus was beginning to look decidedly lumpy. The uniform issued to the driver had evidently worn out. The man at the wheel looked more comfortable in his skull-cap, djellaba, and pointed yellow leather slippers.

It was market day, and the street was a mass of people intent on getting their shopping done before the temperature stoked up. From his blackened cave a grimy charcoal seller blinked like a mole into the blazing sun. Pushing a cart, a weathered fisherman hawked fresh sardines with harsh gutteral cries that seemed to echo the hardship of his profession. Fresh-faced country girls, in red- and white-striped shawls and floppy straw hats, sat primly before piles of home-grown vegetables. The midday heat was intense, and the air was pervaded by the sickly-sweet smell of uncollected garbage. The shouting and the haggling, the swarms of flies and the confusion: it was a scene to send the average American tourist home in a strait-jacket. I didn't mind because I was on the bus.

At the bottom of the Old Mountain, where the road crosses Oued el Ihud, or Jews' River – a parched gully most of the year, a dangerous and destructive current during the rainy season – the bus lurched to a stop. There had been an accident. The passengers scrambled to the windows on my side of the bus to look out. Trailing a skid mark like a black tail, a motorcycle lay on the pavement. Beside it sat a boy with a bloody arm. Jammed up against the curb near the corner of the bridge was a little Morris

Minor with a Spanish license plate. It looked as though the motorcycle had swerved to avoid the on-coming car but nevertheless crashed straight into it.

'Suicide Village' was living up to its name.

The car I recognized immediately. It was Miss Toledano's. The job offer from UNESCO was going to include a Jeep to drive around the Andes Mountains. So she had started driving again, to get some practice. And here she was, involved in an accident already.

Looking down from the bus window directly above the car, I couldn't see her face. Only her red-tipped fingers were visible through the windshield, gripping the wheel. The knuckles were white. The Moroccans pressed so densely around the car that she couldn't open the door.

I jumped down from the bus and made my way through the crowd. They were beginning to rock the car. Two boys had climbed on top.

'You better get down,' I said. 'You'll ruin the paint-job.'

The boys jumped away. Luckily I was about a foot taller than anyone else. The rocking stopped. The crowd drew back and let me through.

I crouched down beside the car and tapped on the window. Miss Toledano's face was rigid, like a mask. When she saw me her expression transformed im-mediately into one of relief. She rolled down the window.

'Norman! Thank God! Where did you come from?'

'I was on the bus.' I squatted down so my face was on a level with hers. 'Are you all right?'

'He came straight at me. I couldn't get out of the way!'

I placed my elbows on the rim of the window. 'Aren't you still a little wild behind the wheel?'

'They're calling me a Jew!' she hissed.

'Maybe you should practice driving somewhere where it's not so crowded.'

'We can't talk about that right now. Go see if the boy is all right.'

'Did you get your international driver's licence?'

Her eyebrows concentrated. The severe expression and black clothes made me think of a flamenco dancer Alice and I had seen perform in Spain.

'I haven't had time!'

'You said your American licence isn't valid in Morocco without the international. If the police come...'

'Just get me out of here before something worse happens!'

I stood up. 'Stay here. I'll be right back.'

'Norman!' she called after me.

I returned to the car. 'What?'

'One of them has a knife!' she whispered. 'Be careful!'

I waded through the crowd to the place where the boy was sitting on the road.

'Are you all right?' I asked.

He showed me his bloody elbow.

'He should go to the hospital!' an angry voice

demanded. 'Someone call an ambulance!'

'It's just a scratch,' another answered.

'She was driving too fast! She was on the wrong side of the road!'

I helped the boy to his feet. 'Let's take a look at your bike.'

We lifted the motorcycle, an old model of Spanish design. I rolled it back and forth and saw that the wheels were aligned. I tested the brakes and clutch.

'I think it's all right.'

The boy pointed to a dent on the fender.

'Make the Jewess pay!' the voice shouted.

His words stirred a grumbling murmur among the Moroccans. Out of the corner of my eye I saw the knife, but so did the others. A blow was landed, and the knife fell on the road.

It was one of those home-made knives, crudely fashioned from the leaf spring of a car, that you see in the fish market. The blade, about a foot long, was ground down to an evil-looking point.

A robed arm snatched it up. A man was subdued in a tumble of djellabas. Moroccans don't fight with their fists; they butt each other like goats. He was dragged away screaming.

Suddenly, the air felt hot. The sight of the knife made my heart pump. I was sweating all over my body. The crowd closed in again with an air of menace.

I straddled the motorcycle. With my toe I found neutral and kicked the thing to life.

'There's nothing wrong with this machine!' I

shouted, revving the motor to full throttle to make the people stand back.

It was lucky I spoke Spanish. A misunderstanding at this point might have led to serious consequences.

'You need to get that arm treated,' I said to the boy. 'You come with me. There's a dispensary up the street. They'll do it for you.'

I shut off the motor and propped the machine on its stand. Picking out an old man in the crowd, I handed him a coin and asked him to look after it. Then I led the boy to the car.

Miss Toledano's eyes grew big when she saw his bloody arm.

'Start the car,' I said. 'Let's get out of here.'

'Is he all right?'

'Probably nothing more than what a little soap and water won't cure.'

I opened the car door. The boy climbed into the back, and I sat in the front seat next to Miss Toledano.

'It might simplify matters if a little money changed hands,' I whispered.

She reached for her purse.

'Not here! Too many people around. Later.'

She started the car, but we still couldn't move. The Moroccans were packed around us, like a human wall.

'They won't let us through!' Miss Toledano's strangulated voice told me she was verging on hysteria.

I placed my hand on her arm. 'Try to stay calm.' I

opened the car door, got out and stood up on the door frame so I was about two feet taller than anybody else.

'We take boy to hospital!' I announced in pidgin Arabic, trying to remember the words Fatima had taught me. 'Doctor see that boy all right! Later, we fix moto. I pay.'

The crowd grudgingly gave way in front of us. We drove slowly to the dispensary, a low white building with the green and red flag of Morocco hanging over the front door. I must have passed it a dozen times with Alice without ever thinking I would have reason to go inside. Here I was lucky again, for the person in charge was Malika, Dr Daniels' nurse. She recognized me from the *clinica* and ushered us inside.

Malika was a stocky, energetic woman, whose crisp white uniform accentuated her nut-brown skin and black hair cut short around her ears. Bouncing around the dispensary like a rubber ball, she cleaned the wound and painted it with disinfectant. When she wrapped the boy's arm in a big snowy bandage, he smiled for the first time.

Miss Toledano was gripping my hand and staring at me with an almost hypnotic intensity. 'I didn't know you spoke Arabic!'

'I don't. Just a few words I learned from Fatima.'

'No, no, it's better than that. When they heard a foreigner speaking their own language, they knew you meant business. They knew you *cared*! That's why they backed off.'

'Do you have any money?' I whispered.

She dug into her purse and handed me a hundred dirham note.

'Don't you have anything smaller?'

'Give it to him!'

We drove the boy back to his motorcycle. The crowd had dispersed. The bus had gone on. The whole incident seemed like a bad dream. A woman was sitting on the curb, rocking and moaning. But her face brightened when she saw that her son was safe. She hugged Miss Toledano, kissing her on both shoulders. She kissed my hand and sleeve, all the while murmuring blessings and thanks in Spanish and Arabic.

'*Merci, gracias,* thank you and your wife.'

Miss Toledano and I looked at each other and laughed. I gave the boy fifty dirhams to repair his motorcycle with, and we got back into the car.

'You saved the day, Norman, their day and mine.'

She leaned over and kissed me on the cheek.

'You were in the right place at the right time – just like that day in Peru.'

Her breath tickled my ear. I could smell her perfume. That was the first time anyone had kissed me since the day – suddenly it seemed like a long time ago – the day Alice bundled me off to the *clinica*.

'I could use a drink after that,' she said. 'A big one. How about you?'

'Sounds good to me.'

'Plus, I have a surprise for you.'

'What is it?'
'Wait and see.'

We drove to the Marshan, a plateau-like area overlooking the sea that is another one of Tangier's
residential districts. Her house I recognized immediately – it was located right across the street from Dr
Daniels' *clinica*.

Like Harry said, it was a big old house, sort of
haunted-looking from neglect, set back from the
street behind a high iron fence that ended with sharp
points along the top. The façade was latticed with
creepers. The paint peeling off the walls gave the
place a mottled, camouflaged look – it had been
painted so many times in so many different colours.
All a long time ago. The iron lace balcony did not
look safe. Vines spiralled up the drainpipes, and
some bushes had taken root in the gutters. The
garden was completely overgrown, and a once-grand
fountain was cracked, lichen-covered and dry.

'When I was sick with asthma and waiting for
Alice to come up,' I said, 'I used to gaze at this house
with the little white car parked outside and wonder
who lived here.'

'Well,' she sighed, 'now you know.'

'I was mesmerized by this place without knowing
why. Then one day the penny dropped. This house
was reminding me of some big, square crumbling
houses I saw in towns on the upper Amazon in Peru.
I was told they were built by Spanish merchants
during the rubber boom. Do you think there's a

connection? I mean, maybe some of your ancestors migrated to Peru after they left Spain.'

Miss Toledano hobbled on ahead without answering.

'I remember thinking, that Morris Minor parked on the drive – it seems too small for such a big house. A house that size needs a Cadillac outside, or a Bentley – even it it's falling down.'

'Well, I'm my brothers' servant and I don't have the time, or the money, or the heart to make any more repairs,' she said sharply.

'I like it the way it is. Run-down places always make me dream of days of glory.'

She led the way to the door. 'Look at this garden. It's a jungle.'

'Just like the Amazon.'

Miss Toledano shot me a resentful glance, which made me understand that I must repress my enthusiasm for the place, since she regarded it as a kind of prison. There were ramps everywhere, presumably for wheelchairs.

We went through a doorway framed by blue and white Spanish tiles. Downstairs was completely empty. Gloomy, high-ceilinged rooms without a stick of furniture. The place smelled of damp. The membranes inside my nose twinged, warning me not to spend the night here. White squares on the walls marked the spaces where pictures had once hung. A marble staircase spiralled upwards toward an oval skylight that let a pale luminosity down into the house.

'What happened to the furniture?' I asked.

'It was sold years ago when we thought we were never coming back.'

Our voices echoed in the cavernous room.

'May I see the key to the house in Spain?' I asked. 'Harry told me about it.'

She went to the mantelpiece and took down a rusty piece of iron. It was about two feet long and looked more like a shovel than a key. You could have dug a trench with it.

'What do you do with this?' I asked. 'I mean, it's not exactly something you put in your pocket when you take the dog for a walk.'

'It was a ceremonial key to the main door where a horse and carriage could pass in and out. There would have been a smaller door in the big door for people to go through. You see, when my ancestors left Granada, they thought they would be coming back. That's why they took the key with them.'

'When was that?'

'1492,' she answered wearily.

'The same year that Columbus discovered America?'

'That also happened to be the year that the Kingdom of Granada fell to the Christian army of Ferdinand and Isabella. The Muslims and Jews had to flee or face being converted to Christianity. Some who refused were burnt alive at the stake.'

A chorus of voices suddenly erupted from another room.

'Slut! Where have you been?'

'Who's that with you?'

'You're late! We want our lunch!'

Miss Toledano gave me a look of resignation. 'Go on up,' she whispered, giving me a little push toward the stairs. 'I'll be with you in a few minutes.'

Stopping halfway up the stairs, I turned around and peered down into the vast empty room below me. It looked like a neglected swimming pool that the water had run out of. The derelict grandeur of the house and the strange stories I had heard about her family brought the realization that I knew hardly anything about Miss Toledano. What kind of person she was, or what kind of secrets she might have. All this history and all this property, and all she wanted was to go back to Peru. She drank too much and she smoked kif; but a divine spark burned inside her, for her idea of freedom from all this was to help another human being.

Upstairs was above tree-level. The sunlight flowed in, making the second floor warmer and drier. My nose stopped tingling. Miss Toledano had created a cozy nest consisting of a bedroom, a kitchen and a living room. Moroccan rugs lay on the floor at different angles, and the walls were hung with paintings by artists with Spanish names whom she must have known when she lived in Madrid.

Besides the daybed in the living room there was a small sofa and two easy chairs austerely upholstered in white Moroccan wool. A gateleg table that served as her desk was set against the wall. A glass-top coffee table completed the simple decor. A low bookshelf held white, hand-cut French paperbacks.

From below came the sound of china breaking.

'To hell with this diet!' a voice shouted. 'While I'm still alive I'm going to eat what pleases me, dammit!'

'Who's that guy with you?'

'That's Norman,' I heard Miss Toledano answer, 'a young American who teaches at the Library.'

'Your hands are shaking, sister. What's wrong with you?'

I crept to the top of the stairs and listened.

'I've just had an accident,' she said.

'Where? What happened?'

'At Jews' River. A boy driving a motorcycle rammed straight into me.'

'Anybody hurt?'

'The boy scraped his arm on the pavement. A bloody scratch, but nothing serious.'

'What about the car?'

'It's all right. But what happened afterwards was terrifying.'

'What?'

'You know what Dradeb is like on market day. No park, no playground, no place to go but the street. A frustrated mob converged on the car and surrounded me. One minute they had been shopping for their families, the next they had murder in their hearts. At first I thought they were just curious, pressing their faces up against the glass, but it quickly got nasty. Someone climbed on top of the car and started jumping on it. They were calling me

"Jew!" I saw a knife. I thought, "My God, they are going to drag me out and cut my throat or turn the car over and set fire to it with me inside." I was trapped! Just then Norman appeared out of nowhere. I was never so glad to see anyone in my life! He was very calm. The crowd didn't unnerve him, or, if it did, he didn't show it. He asked the boys to get off the car, politely, and they did. He asked the people to stand back. They did. The crowd parted before him. He speaks good Spanish and some Arabic. He picked the boy off the pavement and got him into the car. He knows about motorcycles and made sure the motorcycle was all right. We drove the boy to the dispensary. The nurse in charge was a friend of his. She bandaged the boy's arm, and that, believe it or not, was the end of it. But if he hadn't come along, I don't know what might have happened – he may have saved my life!'

Sprinkled about Miss Toledano's living room were the souvenirs of her travels in Peru, each with its spiritual connotation. I recognized a knotted string *quipu*, which the Incas kept their accounts on. There was a Chimu double whistling jar, a star-shaped mace from Titicaca, and a collection of *chuno*, or freeze-dried potatoes. A pot in the shape of a pelican, another in the form of a frog, a face-collar jar from Chiclayo, a bone carving of a man holding a corn cob – the sight and especially the smell of them brought back strong memories of the Andean Indian culture of Peru.

A cat appeared from nowhere and rubbed against my leg.

More noises echoed from below — male voices complaining and pots and pans being banged around. A few minutes later Miss Toledano came upstairs. Her hand trembled as she poured out the gin. She sliced the lime the way they do it in Peru — lengthwise down the side of the core which produces thick seedless chunks you can squeeze a lot of juice out of.

She took out the silver box and lit one of her cigarettes.

'Sure you don't want one?'

'No thanks.'

'Now you see why I smoke kif. It soothes my nerves after being bawled out by two angry men. Come on, I want to show you the surprise I have for you.'

We carried our drinks into the kitchen. A bucket sat on the floor. Thousands of those white worms were swimming around inside.

She lifted the bucket up. '*Hay angulas!*'

She placed the bucket in the sink and turned on the tap.

'Are we going to eat them?'

'*Claro que sí!* But first we have to get rid of the slime.'

'How do you do that?'

'With salt.'

She opened a bag of coarse salt and poured some in. The eels convulsed as one, as though they all belonged to a single living organism, and started swimming frantically.

'What are they doing?'

'The salt makes the slime come out, masses of it. That's why we have to keep the water running.'

The eels were swimming in a frenzy. Some tried to jump out. Then, as suddenly as it had begun, all motion inside the bucket ceased. The eels had expired together. Not a single one was left wiggling.

She turned off the tap, poured the slimy water out of the bucket, and dumped the eels into a colander. While they drained, she heated up olive oil in two miniature clay casseroles on the stove and started chopping garlic on a board. I went back into the living room for the gin bottle.

'Ow! Dammit!' I heard her shout.

I ran back into the kitchen. 'What's wrong?'

She held up a bloody finger.

'My God!'

She had cut the tip of it nearly off chopping garlic. The blood welled up and flowed down her hand.

'Let me hold it!' I shouted.

'Uh uh!' She rolled her eyes but couldn't speak because her finger was in her mouth.

'That won't work! You have to use pressure!'

I pulled her hand from her mouth and pressed the wound shut with my thumb. It took a minute for the bleeding to stop. Both our hands were sticky with blood.

She was pointing toward the drawer in the kitchen table. I pulled it open. It was full of Band-Aids. I peeled one open but couldn't get it to stick because there was so much blood. Each time I let go of her finger more blood spilled out and I had to start all over again.

'Now I understand why you have so many Band-Aids on your fingers,' I said. 'And I thought you had an eczema problem.'

She backed against the table and shut her eyes. The sight of so much blood was making me feel dizzy, too.

At last I got two Band-Aids over the tip of her finger and closed the wound. A third I wrapped tightly around them to keep the blood from leaking out. Bloody Band-Aid wrappers littered the table.

'Now that your blood is all over both of us must mean something,' I said. 'Maybe it means our lives will be intertwined forever.'

She pushed me roughly away with both hands, held me firmly at arm's length, and fixed me with a penetrating scowl.

'Do you think that's true, Norman?' Her voice sounded strangely faint.

'Not if you go to Peru.'

She fell forward and leaned her body against mine. 'I'll be back,' she whispered next to my ear. 'I can't leave them forever.'

'Tangerines always come back, don't they?' I said. 'Even the eels come back.'

She nestled her head against my shoulder. 'Even the Jews come back.'

It took a while for our appetites to return. When the oil was hot, she dropped in the garlic and flakes of the fiery red pepper that the Moroccans call *sudaneeya*. While she worked, Miss Toledano made slurping noises, as she swallowed the saliva that was building up inside her mouth. In anticipation of the feast, she let out little squeals of delight. When the garlic began to sizzle and turn brown, she dropped a handful of eels into each casserole and turned off the gas. The eels cooked instantly in the hot oil. All they required was a stir.

'We have to eat them with a wooden fork,' she said. 'The slippery little devils will slide off a metal one.'

'You eat a lot of garlic, don't you?'

'My mother used to swear by garlic.' Miss Toledano tucked into the eels with exaggerated relish. 'She said it was a vermifuge.'

'What?'

'Worm expeller.'

'It looks to me like you're putting them back in.'

After the effort she had made to prepare them, I hadn't the heart to tell her I didn't think *angulas* had all that much flavour. What taste they do have is overwhelmed by the singed garlic, hot olive oil, and the *sudaneeya*. The eels provide the texture, which is chewy and good.

Even before we finished eating I started to yawn. The combination of gin and lunch was making me groggy. Plus, the incident in Dradeb had taken a lot out of both of us. Miss Toledano suggested a nap. We lay down on her bed, side by side but not touching, and slept for an hour before returning to the Library.

✳

Although Harry continued to give lessons, he admitted he was losing interest in his work. He didn't care much about food either, and seldom finished what was on his plate. Moreover, for long periods of time he remained silent, sunk in thought, almost forgetting that I was seated across the table.

Although I didn't say so, his condition distressed me. Alice had lost her enthusiasm for work, too. And he wasn't looking at all well. His complexion was grey, and he needed a haircut. Sometimes he would forget to put on a necktie, but what I missed most was the sight of his old Spanish briefcase. It used to signify that Harry was still in business.

His conversation, meanwhile, turned more and more gloomy.

'All around the world, situations are developing that sooner or later will affect people sound asleep in their beds. People like you and me, Norman, who've only been hearing about how the world is being defiled by greed and need. Every time I see another article in the newspaper about the rainforest being cut down or the sea turtles being wiped out, I turn the page. I can't bear to read about it, it's so shameful. More and more people are clamouring for a piece of the world's purity – you know, its clean air and its water – and every day there is less of it to go around.'

I told him that when I thought about how the world was going, I often became depressed, too. I tried to turn off the world and concentrate on a personal future, not the world's. It helped a little.

'But that's precisely the point I'm trying to make, Norman. The world's future will soon land right in our laps. It's going to rouse us sleepers any minute. Believe me, it's going to be a rude awakening.'

'Maybe the human race will wake up and turn over a new leaf just in time.'

'History tells us that humanity learns the hard way, after the field is littered with corpses,' Harry said. 'My only purpose in life is to get that tombstone erected. After that I don't care. Next to death everything is emptiness and humbug. A footloose, capricious modernity is not for me.'

One evening he failed to show up at the restaurant. The next morning I waited outside the cemetery, but he didn't turn up there, either. That worried me – he made a point of visiting his mother's grave every day.

Having dropped him off several times at night, I knew by now where Harry lived. Mohamed drove me there. For the first time I got a good look at his building by daylight. It stood by itself in an empty lot where sheep grazed. The area had been taken over by squatters. They had erected shacks made of oilcans beaten flat and sewn together with wire. The roofs were weighed down by stones and old rubber tires. According to Harry, the whole area was about to be bulldozed to make way for a new highway.

Barefoot boys were kicking a ball among newspapers and plastic bags blowing in the wind. The ground floor of the building had been designed as a series of shops – all boarded up and empty now. A number of cats slunk about, followed by emaciated kittens. I climbed the stairs and found his apartment. On the door was a brass plaque:

HARRY BURGE

IDIOMAS Y TRADUCCIONES

The door was locked. I knocked and whispered his name, but no one answered. Even so, I had a funny feeling he was inside. I thought about contacting the landlord but remembered that Harry didn't like him and wouldn't want him in his apartment for any reason.

I went back to the car where Mohamed was waiting and took a pack of celluloid playing cards from the glove compartment. Alice and I used to play gin rummy when there was nothing else to do. Climbing the stairs once more, I took out two of the cards and, pressing them together, slowly inserted them into the crack between the door frame and the door, opposite the lock. It was a trick Alice had taught me the time we'd got drunk and locked ourselves out of our hotel room in the middle of the night. The cards eased the plunger back, and the door opened. It was a good trick.

I stood still for a minute while my eyes adjusted to the gloom. A damp, mouldy odour hung about the place. Stacks of newspapers, waist high, lined the walls of the room. Miss Toledano had mentioned that Harry scavenged old newspapers from the wastebaskets of the American Library. I hadn't known whether to believe it at the time but, judging from the piles of them, I suppose it was true. Some of the newspapers were printed in Spanish and French. Harry was quite a linguist.

Against one wall stood an old sofa with its springs broken right down to the floor, as though someone had been sleeping on it for a long time. The only other piece of furniture was a desk, also piled high with paper. And there sat his Spanish briefcase. The closet door was open. Within I could distinguish the outline of a sink. There was the sound of water dripping. A bucket had overflowed, and a stain of water was spreading across the floor. So this is where Harry lives, I thought.

I was somewhat afraid, I admit. It was so dark and quiet. To intrude on another person's privacy gave me an uncomfortable feeling. Seeing that no one was about, I breathed a sigh of relief. I guess I had been expecting the worst. I was about to leave when I noticed another door on my left. It was shut, but a ribbon of light marked its base. I crossed the room and opened it.

This must have been his mother's room. It was brighter and had a feminine air about it. A blue velvet easy chair with matching footrest was bathed in light from the window. A bird feeder was attached to the shutter. Most likely this was where Mrs Burge spent much of her time, waiting for Harry to return from his lessons. On one side of the room was a bed. On it lay a hand-knitted mauve afghan, neatly folded.

The room made me think of historic houses that Alice and I had visited in England, where the rooms have been maintained in their original state to give visitors an idea of how people used to live. In greater splendour than they do today. In like manner Harry, who lived in comparative squalor next door, was preserving the order of his mother's room. A set of ivory-backed brushes was laid out on the dresser. The carpet had an oriental design. The portrait above the bed looked distorted; it had been executed by an artist struggling with the influence of Picasso. Harry had mentioned that one of his students had been a young Spanish painter too poor to pay for his lessons in cash. Nevertheless, the canvas managed to convey the impression of mutual devotion between a severe, mustachioed young man in wire-rimmed glasses and a three-piece suit, and his mother, whose whimsical expression was accentuated by a straw hat which she wore at a jaunty angle. A watch chain looped between the pockets of his vest gave Harry a surprisingly prosperous look.

I was about to leave when I noticed yet another room whose door stood half open. I glanced inside. It was the bathroom. As I turned away, something moving in the bath tub caught my eye. I pushed the door back for a better view. Harry was lying in the bottom of the tub. He was naked. The water had run out. He was dead.

A sudden movement startled me. A tiny sparrow, which had been sitting on his head, darted up and was trying to find its way out of the bathroom. It circled in a panic before colliding with the window. Stunned, it fell on the floor. I closed my hands gently around it. It couldn't have weighed more than half an ounce and was trembling with terror. Through the feathers I could feel the tiny heartbeat. My hands were shaking, too. I opened the window and put it outside, and it flew away.

On my way out I heard a rustling noise from a wooden box on the floor. I went over and looked down at two tortoises moving slowly on their bed of newspapers and soggy lettuce leaves. On the window sill sat a wrinkled tomato. I broke it open and gave it to them. Wiping my hands on my trousers, I closed the door and went out.

It was a windy day. For a minute I took in the quick movements of the young soccer players against the whitewashed shacks. In their shouts, as they fought for the ball, I detected a querulous note which struck me as a sure sign that they would struggle and survive. Their voices were not unlike the plaintive cries of a solitary, snow-white seagull that was drifting upwards into the blue translucency of space.

Mohamed was convinced it was Harry's soul that had flown away.

※

This time I wanted to do everything right, but I couldn't have managed without Miss Toledano. When you bury somebody for the first time, there are a number of essential details you might overlook. To begin with, I didn't know where the funeral parlour was located. Miss Toledano did. We drove there and informed a pale little Spaniard that our friend had passed away. He handed me some papers to fill out. Next we had to choose the coffin. He led us down to the cellar where several models were on display – everything from a simple pine box to ornate mahogany caskets with red satin linings. As Harry would have objected to any extravagance in this department, I chose the pine box. The under-taker frowned; evidently he considered me to be a tightwad. Did we want a brass plaque engraved with the deceased's name? Fifty dollars seemed like a lot of money for a plaque, but yes, we did. And when would the funeral take place? The weather was unseasonably hot. We decided on the next day.

We found Dr Gomez and persuaded him, against his wishes, to come with us to see the body and sign the death certificate. He took the news of Harry's death without comment, but the whole way over he never stopped complaining what a nuisance it had been to visit Mrs Burge, and how Harry never had enough cash to pay in full.

'Harry was a dear friend of ours,' Miss Toledano told him. 'It's unseemly of you, the family doctor, to speak that way about the dead.'

I admired her for having the gumption to say those words. I could have added that, if he had come the night Mrs Burge died, as he promised, she might be alive today and so, for that matter, might Harry. I could have also reminded him that he wasn't a proper doctor and had received dozens of free English lessons for his services.

As I still didn't have a key, I had to use the card trick again. The doctor watched suspiciously. He took one look at Harry and entered 'heart attack' on the death certificate. Together we lifted him from the tub and lay him on his mother's bed. The doctor had a rope with him. To my dismay he roughly strapped Harry's arms to the sides of his body and bound his legs together, explaining that otherwise he wouldn't fit into the coffin. I wasn't familiar with such procedures so I didn't say anything, but to me it seemed he was binding him with a vengeance. Miss Toledano couldn't look; she was crying softly by the window as she filled the bird feeder. A little trickle of blood spilled from the corner of Harry's mouth. I found his passport and keys and took them with me. Miss Toledano carried the turtles.

After dropping the doctor off we returned to the funeral parlour with the passport so the undertaker could have Harry's name correctly inscribed on the brass plaque, along with the dates of his life.

In the street we ran into Brahim, the taxi driver who gave me a lift the night I returned from New York. Word that Harry had died was already out, as Mohamed had somehow found the opportunity to inform his friends. Tears came to Brahim's eyes when he saw us. He wanted to know when the funeral would take place, and where, and offered his taxi to take friends to the cemetery. All of a sudden he grabbed my hand and squeezed it in both of his. That unexpected gesture got me trembling, and Miss

Toledano was crying again. I asked her to wait in the car while I settled things with the undertaker, who wanted to be paid in advance.

Neither Miss Toledano nor I could recall ever having heard Harry speak of family members he might have somewhere in the world. While she made coffee I telephoned the British Consulate to find out if Harry had left the name of someone to notify. The voice on the other end of the line, whose clipped English accent seemed to imply that any unpleasantness, even death, couldn't be all that bad, asked me to hang on. While I waited, I watched Miss Toledano's cat watching the tortoises nibble the fresh lettuce leaves in the nest she had made for them. Harry said they live for many years. With the exception of men who make guitars from their shells, they have few natural enemies.

The voice came back to say that the person to be notified in case of death was his mother.

'But she's dead, too,' I said.

As Miss Toledano had lived for several years in Tangier, she was no stranger to European death formalities. We did not know if a will existed but, with no relative on hand to claim inheritance, Harry's apartment and all his possessions, she told me, automatically fell into 'vacant succession.' No one was permitted by law to touch anything that belonged to him. Even taking the turtles away was technically illegal.

Mohamed drove us to the municipal authorities. Without a document that could only be obtained

from an office deep in the medina the body, according to the undertaker, could not be transported to the
cemetery. Several people were loitering about.
Waiting means nothing to Moroccans. They do it
their whole lives. It's part of their culture. They
don't have the same feelings about time that we do.

We were admitted to the office of a burly official
who seemed to dislike foreigners. In a gruff voice he
announced that the body could only be transported
in a steel box which could be obtained in Casablanca
for a thousand dollars. I didn't believe this to be true
and suspected the fellow was attempting in his crude
way to extort some money from us. Under the
circumstances he probably figured it would be an
easy thing to do.

'That is the law,' he concluded.

I told him I'd never heard of such a law.

'There are no doubt many laws of my country
that you know nothing about,' he retorted, flexing
his muscles, 'but that doesn't mean you mustn't obey
each and every one of them.'

Mohamed was infuriated by such nonsense and
began to argue with the man in Arabic. There was
no telling what words passed between them, but I
saw that the official, who was twice as big as
Mohamed, was getting the better of it.

'It's hot,' I said. 'The body is already beginning to
smell.'

'All the more reason for the steel box,' was his
reply. 'To prevent the spread of diseases.'

I said there was no disease.

'And if he was sick,' he went on, paying no attention to anything I said, 'why didn't you transport him directly to the hospital, where there are no problems concerning the dead?'

I waved the death certificate in front of his nose.

'Don't you see? It's clearly marked "heart attack"!' I almost shouted. 'These things happen all of a sudden. There's no warning!'

'Was that the real reason?' the man asked suspiciously. 'Have the police seen the body?'

It gave me a scare when he said that. The way Dr Gomez had so roughly strapped him, it might appear that Harry had been a victim of foul play. Many circumstances had contributed to his death, but I didn't want to go into them. When I didn't answer, the man folded his thick arms across his chest and nodded in a knowing way he hoped we would interpret as being threatening or sinister.

I had been in Morocco long enough to observe that Moroccans take a sensible attitude toward death. They don't turn it into an expensive, complicated affair like we do. The body is buried in a shallow grave without undue ceremony, often within hours of death. Coffins are not used. The body is washed, wrapped in a sheet, and carried on a stretcher to the nearest cemetery by friends and relatives, who take turns if the day is hot or the road is far. In Marrakesh, Moktar and I had followed a funeral procession in his carriage. It was a ceremony I had been curious to know about. Muslims are supposed to be buried with their heads toward Mecca, but sometimes, he told me, not even this is done. The body is something to dispose of as quickly as possible, especially in hot weather. The Moroccans exit from the cemetery, not with tears in their eyes but with smiles on their faces. Their duty is done, and their friend is safely in the hands of Allah. I was trying to explain this to the official and repeated that, in effect, all I wanted was to see my friend put into the ground in the simplest possible manner, following the example of his own people, when his superior entered the room.

He was a stately, bearded old fellow who walked with a cane. White robes trailed from behind. I repeated my story. The funeral had already been arranged for tomorrow, I added. We didn't want to make any difficulties. My friend was dead of natural causes. The death certificate said so. He had to be buried. While I was talking, the bully got up and walked out, composed and indifferent, as though he'd never had anything to do with it. The old gentleman nodded, stamped the paper and signed. Rising to his feet, he shook our hands and expressed his sympathies. We thanked him and walked out of the office like free men.

'You were brilliant, Norman!' Miss Toledano said.

'My Spanish got completely garbled trying to explain.'

'I understood every word.'

'I should have let you do the talking. Your Spanish is ten times better than mine.'

'No. It's better they hear it from a man.'

Mohamed was indignant over the shameful behaviour of the bully, who he identified as a police agent from Casablanca. He hadn't even belonged in the old man's office; he just happened to be occupying his chair because the day was hot. He was known all over Tangier, and everybody hated him.

Mohamed and Brahim insisted on standing guard outside Harry's door during the night. I thought it was unnecessary, but they were determined to do it. When someone dies, they explained, thieves move around in the dark in the hope of making off with the possessions of the deceased. Nothing attracts thieves like a corpse. This is particularly true when no next of kin is present to defend the house. So Fatima filled a basket with bread, tomatoes, onions, cheese, olives and so forth, and covered it with a white cloth. They took along a flashlight, a lantern, and two heavy clubs, just in case.

I didn't sleep well that night. Two owls kept calling to each other in the garden. Finally I got up and turned on the light. Fatima heard me moving around. She got up and brewed some thyme tea which makes me sleep. We had our customary chat in the kitchen. The trip to Fez had been a success, she told me. Her niece's complexion was better. What's more, she had gone on a diet and lost some weight. The telephone company had given her a raise. A young man had started coming around to the house. A marriage was being arranged between the two families.

✳

At first light I rose from my bed and wandered onto the terrace to have a look at the dawn. An owl flew soundlessly through the trees to join its mate. The neighbour's cat was returning from a night of hunting in the garden. The stealth of its step, the grace of the owl's flight, the deep shadow of the woods where pockets of night still lingered, and above all the astonishing quantity of light that was pouring across the watery horizon between the Pillars of Hercules — it was all so silent, so wild and mysterious that I didn't dare move. I could have watched it forever because I liked being part of it.

Although I hadn't slept much, I felt prepared for what lay ahead. I showered and shaved and put on my only suit. Mohamed turned up to drive me into town. We picked up Miss Toledano at her home. As she came down the steps I was struck by her Mediterranean beauty. Spanish women know how to wear black. The colour lends them gravity and elegance. Through her veil her face looked mysterious.

It was market day, and country women were coming into Tangier carrying bunches of fresh flowers. We bought them by the armful. Everyone in the market knew of Harry's death, as word had passed quickly. Information is exchanged more quickly in a native market than we do over the telephone. The egg lady, the fish vendor, the man who sold cornflakes — they all left their stalls to offer their condolences. Harry had many friends in Tangier, people of all classes and nationalities. He had shopped for his mother and himself in this market. They knew what kind of food he liked and considered him to be one of their own, that is, a Tangerine. And like all Tangerines he would be missed and nobody could replace him. The flower ladies, meanwhile, were adding irises and gladioli to the pile I'd already paid for. In the end we had to hire another taxi just to carry the flowers.

The hearse, an ancient wooden vehicle with carved black angels for decoration, was already parked in front of Harry's building. The grave diggers in their rough grey uniforms and black hats were waiting, along with the undertaker and a young, suntanned English priest.

Two policemen stood with their hands behind their backs, speaking in hushed tones. Brahim, club in hand, respectfully guarded the door. He wasn't going to let anyone in, not even the policemen, until we arrived.

The coffin was carried upstairs and placed on sawhorses beside the bed. A tattered black cloth with a white cross emblazoned on it was draped over the coffin. Evidently the undertaker was making no further investment in his business. I thought it was a poor show. Moth holes did not lend dignity to the occasion.

While everybody stood silently the priest said a few words. This was followed by a moment of indecision when it was discovered that Harry lay stark naked beneath the afghan. The manner in which his arms and legs had been so rudely bound did convey the impression of foul play. He had also bled a lot more from the mouth. The policemen stepped forward to take a closer look. I explained that the doctor had tied him like that so he would fit in the coffin. The undertaker, who was anxious to finish the job, affirmed that it was normal procedure. I gave the order for Harry to be buried in his mother's afghan, beautiful as it was. Nobody else would be using it. So we lifted him in the afghan and placed him in the coffin. While the lid was screwed down, the priest spoke a few more words. I resented his suntan; it didn't seem right for a priest, especially on such a solemn occasion.

I wondered if I should make a quick search through Harry's papers for a will, but the policemen were signalling for everyone to leave.

'Take something, Norman!' Miss Toledano whispered.

'I thought it was against the law.'

'Something to remember him by. He would want you to.'

I picked up Harry's old briefcase.

'Good, Norman, good.'

The policemen shut the door, locked it, and sealed it with lead and wire. There was no telling when, if ever, that door would be opened again, or by whom.

✳

To the consternation of the undertaker, I commanded the driver of the hearse to go slowly. We made a small procession through the town. The Spanish people in the street doffed their hats and made the sign of the cross as we went by.

A crowd had gathered outside the cemetery. I recognized the faces of Harry's colleagues from the Spanish Institute. Spectral shadows of their former selves, they made no secret of the fact that they would soon be joining their friend. Penniless and out of work but desiring to go nowhere else, they were hanging on in Tangier, passing their time in cafés and attending one another's funerals. As more mourners arrived in taxis or on foot, they shook hands and mumbled solemn greetings. A dignified, grey-suited gentleman stood with his chauffeur before a large black automobile – the Consul General of Great Britain. And of course there was Mohamed and Fatima and our friend Brahim.

The gate opened and the hearse went in. The priest herded us along like sheep. Located on a hillside, Tangier's International Cemetery is different from the one in Queens. The Spanish prefer to bury their dead in houses, and some were so old that their roofs had fallen in. The walls were blotchy with lichens and moss, and one could only read with difficulty the names of those whose remains were contained within. Faded brown photographs of the deceased peered sadly from weed-grown niches.

Some graves were in a better condition. Potted geraniums had been freshly watered. Miniature gardens being tended by faithful relatives made me wonder if Alice's grave in Queens was receiving the same kind of attention. Cypress trees grew along the paths.

At the graveside I helped unload the coffin. It was placed on the sawhorses once more and the moth-eaten cloth draped over it. While the priest intoned the parting words, my eyes travelled down a row of crosses and came to rest on Mrs Burge's grave, marked by a simple but handsome headstone. Only a few days ago Harry had personally supervised its placement. It was a pity they couldn't have been buried side by side, the way entire Spanish families are, but the graves of strangers separated those of mother and son.

When the moment came to lower the coffin into the pit, Mohamed and Brahim took the ropes from the gravediggers. They wanted to be the ones to set Harry in his final resting place, which they did, slowly and gently, despite the weight of the coffin. Miss Toledano clung to my arm as it dropped out of sight, but not before I noticed that a brass plaque had not been attached to the coffin lid, but a mere strip of plastic.

My first instinct was to take up the matter with the undertaker afterwards, but by then it would have been too late, and he would have succeeded with his deception. Under the circumstances, it seemed futile to squabble over such a detail. After all, who would see it once the hole was filled with earth? Yet I'd had my fill of being taken advantage of by people who figured they could get away with it because I was unhappy.

'Hold on a minute!' I went over to the undertaker. 'Where's that brass plaque?'

He stumbled backwards among the broken clods of dirt. I took him by the arm and led him to the edge of the pit.

'Haul that thing up again!' I said to Mohamed. It was scandalous, I admit, and everyone was gaping. Probably they thought I'd gone mad, but I had promised myself I'd do everything right, and plastic hadn't been part of my design.

The priest came over. 'What's the trouble?' he asked, jutting out his chin.

'I'm sorry, father, but this man has cheated me.' With the coffin resting on the sawhorses once more, I pointed to the strip of plastic. 'I paid for brass, and he gave me plastic!'

The undertaker, who looked like a rodent in distress, was darting his eyes about.

'I have half a mind to push him into the pit and throw the coffin on top of him!'

I never would have done it, of course, but the undertaker must have understood my threat, because he tried to hide behind the priest. The more scared he looked, the angrier I became. And composed. I knew I was right, and it felt good.

The undertaker mumbled something about the plaque not being ready in time.

'Oh, no, you don't! I was afraid that something like this might happen.' I pulled the receipt from my pocket and waved it in front of his nose. 'You made the suggestion, and I ordered it. Now where is it?'

'Calm down,' said the priest. 'For God's sake.'

'I am calm! It was his idea in the first place. He

even insinuated that if I didn't, I'd be a cheapskate, not generous toward my friend. Look here. That's almost fifty dollars.' I showed him the receipt. 'I see what he was up to now, father. He made sure the coffin was covered with that moth-eaten rag right up to the last minute, hoping we wouldn't notice. And if we did notice, I bet he calculated that we'd be so overcome with sorrow or anxious to get the whole thing over with that we wouldn't care if it was plastic or brass!'

'Please restrain yourself!' The priest was worried about what other people might think.

'Excuse me, father. You may think this is a petty thing to squabble over, but I did notice, and I do care! Harry would have cared, too. If he weren't in that box, he'd stand up and give this fellow a punch in the nose. I bet he plays the same trick on everybody!'

The priest patted my hand and showed me his profile. His ears stuck out from the sides of his head like dried apricots. For my money, he was spending too much time in the sun. He was the one who had kept Harry's mother out of the English Cemetery. I didn't like him.

'Leave everything to me,' he said, modulating his voice. 'I'll see what I can do.'

He took the undertaker aside. After a brief discussion he went off.

'You may talk now,' the priest said condescendingly, as though we were all a bunch of imbeciles. 'Please act naturally.'

We had to wait nearly an hour. The interruption altered the mood of the occasion. People stood around chatting in the sun. You could have put drinks in our hands, and the scene would have resembled a garden party.

At last the undertaker came back with the brass plaque and screwed it to the coffin lid. But it still didn't look right to me. It wasn't shiny. I stepped forward for a better look.

HARRY BURGE
IDIOMAS Y TRADUCCIONES

'Hey, this isn't what I ordered. He took this off Harry's door!'

'Please,' the priest pleaded. 'We must conclude the ceremony.'

'He's still cheating me. You're in charge here. He shouldn't be allowed to get away with it.'

'We must continue.'

'All right, but I want my money back.'

The ceremony began all over again. Once more the priest intoned the parting words. For the final time the coffin was lowered into the grave. Handkerchiefs were out like little flags of farewell. Stepping forward, Miss Toledano picked up a handful of earth and dropped it into the hole. It was another thing I would never have thought of. I followed her example, and so did everyone else.

As we drifted away from the grave, the diggers began to rain shovelfuls of earth onto the coffin, which reverberated with eerie, hollow thuds, like the sound of someone pounding from within. I went back and asked them to hold off until we were out of ear-shot. They leaned on their shovels and lit cigarettes while the undertaker paced nervously back and forth.

At the gate everyone was saying goodbye. The British Consul drove away in his big car without offering anyone a lift. Harry's old colleagues trudged off under the blazing sun or waited for the bus back to town. Mohamed and Fatima helped carry the flowers to the grave. The diggers had filled it in and left a little mound of dirt on top. In time the ground would settle, and the earth would return to its green and grassy state. Then the headstone could be set in place.

One of Miss Toledano's specialities was flower arranging. The result was pretty, but one might have concluded that it was a waste of so many flowers. Only the day before they had been blossoming in mountain pastures. Many were already wilting in the hot North African sun.

I had been sweating in my dark suit and was feeling a little dizzy from standing so long in the sun. I was grateful, therefore, when Miss Toledano invited me to her home for lunch. Mohamed dropped us off in the car. The tall trees shading her house provided a welcome relief from the heat. Suddenly I felt like I needed to be alone.

'Are you all right, Norman?'

'I think I'll stay in the garden for a few minutes and cool off.'

I found a bench and brushed away the leaves. I don't cry easily. Something prevents my tear ducts from opening, even when I want them to. I think I got anaesthetized at an early age, when my family disintegrated. My father moved out of the house and the fighting stopped; but in the resulting silence the hurt, the bewilderment, and the unexpressed grief burrowed deep inside and stayed there. As a result, my emotions don't seep out very often.

But after the intense heat of the cemetery, the shadowy coolness of the garden caressed me like a mother's hand, and my tears came.

I felt better afterwards but didn't have the energy to move. I stayed on the bench and listened to the birds. The trees in Miss Toledano's garden are alive with them. Other small creatures were scurrying in the bushes. A frog croaked somewhere. A gecko, its tail missing, clung to a palm tree and watched me with agate eyes.

Harry's body was in the International Cemetery – I was in no doubt about that. But did some vital essence of him still exist somewhere? I hoped so. Like that sparrow whose feet were entangled in his hair, had his soul flown to some permanent place whose existence we can only guess at? Or is that just wishful thinking? Harry told me about an article he'd read in *Scientific American* that predicted the existence of a parallel universe which, in death, we all jump into and start up another life. Far-fetched as that may sound, to me it is just as plausible as the idea of heaven or hell. And the birds that flit through

Miss Toledano's garden – they must own souls, too. And so must frogs and worms and other wet creatures we don't normally keep as pets. Either they do, or we don't. There can't be anything in between. If we go somewhere in death, the animals are coming with us. After all, Noah made sure that no creature got left off the Ark. In Peru I learned that forest Indians worship trees, especially big trees, because they believe spirits inhabit them. People who spend their whole lives out of doors know more about these things than we do.

✳

One of Miss Toledano's brothers was waiting for me by the door. He wasn't the emaciated, sickly invalid I had imagined. If anything he looked a little over-weight. He suffered from a severe case of lordosis, which bent his body so far over in his wheelchair that about all I could see of him was the top of his head. A yarmulka partially covered a bald spot.

'My sister says you're from New York,' he said, speaking hoarsely into his lap.

'New Jersey, actually.'

'New Jersey . . .' He repeated the words slowly, as though they were the name of a foreign country. 'My uncle used to have a place at Mountain Lakes.'

'I know Mountain Lakes. My father used to take me fishing up there.'

With difficulty he lifted his eyes to mine. His face was triangular, his eyes almond-shaped like his sister's. A little black beard stuck out from the end of his chin.

'I'm sorry about Harry,' he whispered. 'You were his friend.'

'You should have come to the funeral.'

'That International Cemetery is uphill all the way.'

'It must be tough getting around in that thing. Someone would have pushed you.'

'I don't want anyone pushing. Here, I have something for you...' His hand groped toward his pocket. 'My sister told us about what happened at Jews' River.'

'Well, it was unexpected. I've never seen the Moroccans behave like that.'

'There's a reason – everything has a reason.'

'What is it?'

'It was on the news the night before that the Israelis had killed twelve Arabs in a commando raid. That's what got everybody stirred up. I'm told the cafés in Tangier were full, with everyone glued to the television ... What followed were reprisals against Jews all over Morocco, even though the Sultan has proclaimed us officially welcome here. In Meknès an old man was pushed in front of a taxi and killed.'

'I'm sorry. I suppose I should buy a TV and stay in touch.'

'This isn't New Jersey, my friend. In Morocco you only hear about these cruelties by word of mouth. A cousin called from Casablanca to say that some boys beat up an American tourist right in front of his hotel because they thought he looked like a Jew.'

'I guess it was just lucky I happened to be on that bus. Anything could have happened.'

'Jews' River has a special significance for our family. Did my sister tell you that?'

'No.'

'It's the spot where our ancestors came ashore in Morocco after they were chased out of Spain. That's how the place got its name. Their lives were saved in that place, and now you've saved us again.'

It took him another minute to fish something out of his pocket. His hand drifted unsteadily toward me. The fingers opened in slow motion, like a flower. In his palm lay a gold pocket watch surrounded by a nest of golden chain.

'You know Harry was always afraid of being mugged in that neighbourhood he lived in. He left this with us for safekeeping.'

'This is too valuable for me.' I picked the watch from his outstretched palm. 'I'll probably lose it.'

'You saved our sister's life. We want you to have it.'

I turned the watch over in my hand. On the back the words *Je t'aime* were inscribed.

'Is this the watch Harry is wearing in the painting above his mother's bed?'

'Mrs. Burge ordered it from New York and gave it to him on his twenty-first birthday.'

I placed the watch against my ear. It had stopped ticking.

*

Miss Toledano always had something delicious on the stove or in the fridge – smelly things like goats cheese, anchovy fillets in olive oil, and chickpeas flavoured with garlic and fierce spices from the souk. As usual, gin and tonics followed by a heavy lunch on a hot day made me so sleepy I could hardly keep my eyes open. I asked if she minded if I took a nap. She turned on the fan and went around the room closing the shutters while I took off my jacket and shoes and lay down on her bed.

I woke up feeling sluggish from the alcohol I'd drunk. I'd also had a heavy dream which left me feeling anxious without knowing the reason why.

I stayed on the bed without moving as the fan swung back and forth. I must have slept for a couple of hours, because the bands of sunlight filtering through the shutters laddered the floor in different places. The shrill cries of children playing in the park across the street pierced the hot silence of the North African afternoon. Every few seconds my face was brushed by a cooling breeze from the fan.

While I lay there the dream came back.

A woman with my mother's voice was yelling at me. Without waiting to hear what she wanted, I jumped, notebook in hand, from some bushes where I had been hiding and ran down the street. The scene was New York. I was about to enter a tall building when I realized I was barefoot. I ducked into a shoe store, where a sleazy salesman persuaded me to buy a pair of 'Barcelona loafers' – shoes with the ends cut off so my toes showed. Only half a sole and no heel. I reeled at the price – ninety-five dollars – but forked over the money.

As I entered the building I noticed that my

trousers were covered with oil stains from my motor-cycle. The young receptionist tittered at my appearance. I went upstairs to meet the editor, a young, bespectacled preppie dressed in tweeds. I handed him the notebook, and he began to read. I showed him another notebook I had with me. It was bound in plastic and looked like a second-hand cookbook. 'I read that,' he said. 'It's disgusting.' He read on. 'This is disgusting,' he said. He read on. End of dream.

I didn't dare move because Miss Toledano lay sound asleep by my side. She had taken off her black clothes and put on a sand-coloured Moroccan robe. Under it I could make out the contours of her body. Pale blue embroidery webbed the collar and sleeves. I watched her for a while. You can learn things about people when they're asleep. You are able to study them closely without disturbing them and divine all sorts of truths. I was mesmerized by Miss Toledano's dark-skinned body so close to mine. She had a kind of grave, old world beauty you see on Greek pottery and Roman death masks. Even in sleep a troubled expression never left her face,. The scowl wasn't there, but it had left a permanent vertical crease between her eyebrows, like a scar.

I had never seen her hair before. It lay in a thick spray across the pillow. I rolled my head nearer. With my face close to hers she opened her eyes and smiled.

'I was just smelling your hair,' I said. 'Why do you keep it hidden?'

'You know what the wind is like in Tangier,' she

said, arching her back against the bed and stretching. 'When the *levante* comes, it blows for three, six or even nine days. That's why I keep my hair covered. Otherwise, it would be all over my face.'

With our faces just inches apart on the pillow it seemed natural to kiss. Little kisses that became stronger. I slipped my arm around her and pulled her closer. Our bodies clipped together like magnets. She explored my back with her fingers, digging them in like a cat testing its claws. Through my shirt I could feel the prick of her nails.

'Do you think Harry can see us now?' I asked.

'I don't know. Do you think he'd be jealous?'

'Maybe, but I don't think he'd be surprised.'

As we lay there on top of the bed, our bodies bathed by the breeze from the fan, I told her about my dream.

'Have you always kept a diary?' she asked.

'It started off as a list of expenses. In Peru I was keeping myself on a strict budget to make my money go farther. I'd write down in a notebook what I had paid for lunch, the price of my hotel room, a bus ticket and so forth, then add it up at the end of the day. Then, for nothing better to do at mealtimes, since I always ate alone, I began making notes about what I ate. I listed what I thought were the ingredients, sometimes consulting the waiter to see if I had got them right. *Ceviche*, for instance.'

'That's my favourite dish!'

'I was eating most of my meals in Indian restaurants because they were so much cheaper. I thought, well, maybe I ought to write a cookbook about Peruvian food. To my mind, it's one of the great unsung cuisines of the world.'

'How right you are! What a good idea.'

'One night in Lima the waiter who was clearing away the plates mumbled, "It's raining and the canaries are dying." It didn't make any sense, but it was a vivid image, so I wrote it down. Things like that. That's how my diary got going. And when I went out into the street it was raining.'

'It never rains in Lima! There's only that stinking *garua*!'

'Well, it was raining that night, but I didn't see any dead canaries.'

She snuggled closer. 'Do you want to be a writer, Norman?'

'I just don't want everything to be forgotten, which is so easy to do when you're alone.'

She sighed. 'Alone with no one to share your memories.'

'That's right. By putting down on paper descriptions of what I'd seen or done, I was able to give some form to the formless life I was leading. Writing things down reassured me. It clarified my thoughts. It also gave me something to do when I was alone. It built up my confidence in a foreign land. My diary became a companion that I looked forward to communing with every day. Now I have a pile of notebooks with my memories made permanent inside. I can refer to them any time I want, like a private encyclopaedia.'

We stayed on the bed, our arms and legs inter-twined, while the room filled with shadows. I spent the whole night with Miss Toledano. It was lovely. At five o'clock in the morning I woke up feeling released from tension. I slipped out of bed without waking her and dressed. Letting myself out of the house, I walked down to Merkala for a swim. At that hour the beach is totally deserted. Feeling light, as though a stone had been lifted from my shoulders, I submerged myself in the water while the sun rose over the Strait of Gibraltar.

That swim turned out to be a bad idea. The water was ice cold and I didn't have a towel to give myself a proper 'friction,' as the doctor advised. I caught a chill and the next night I had a bad attack.

Luckily Miss Toledano came right away when it started. I instructed her to prepare an injection that I keep for emergencies. She was very much afraid seeing me in such a state – gasping for breath, gripping the sides of the bed, the sweat pouring off me in big drops. An acute attack, especially after dark, can be an unnerving experience for both patient and witness. She had never given an injection before and was fearful of giving me an overdose, lest I have a heart attack and die. I watched her prepare the syringe and begged her to hurry. My eyes must have been popping out of my head, I wanted that shot so badly. Her hands were shaking, and she cut herself trying to open one of those little glass vials the adrenaline comes in. There was blood all over everything. In the end she administered only half the necessary dose without telling me. When it became apparent that it was to have no effect, I was sure I was finished, for adrenaline had always given me relief in the past.

Finally she drove me to the Italian Hospital where the nuns housed me in an oxygen tent. She brought soup to revive me.

Miss Toledano's way of making soup is to go to market and buy the oldest and toughest bird she can find. She takes it to the chicken killer and waits, eyes averted, while he chops off the head, feathers and guts this mother of roosters. She boils the bird all day before fishing the carcass out of the pot and giving it to the cat. With the resulting broth and numerous hot toddies she nursed me back to life.

I wasn't the only one she ministered to. She typed letters for an American lady novelist whose sight was failing, and spent two nights a week with a lonely old English widow who lived down the road from me on the Mountain. She was very popular, always busy, forever being invited out. Miss Toledano was in such demand that sometimes the only way to see her was to creep into the widow's garden at three o'clock in the morning and throw pebbles at her window. She would come downstairs in her bath-robe, open the door and let me hug her warm, pliant, and unresisting body; but she wouldn't let me into the house.

There was a quiet, middle-class Spanish family in Tangier she felt cozy with. She dined with them on a regular basis. Did she find in their company, I wondered, a sense of security that was otherwise lacking in her vagabond life? For me the frustrating thing about these boring soirées was that she put them on an equal footing with our love-making which, once it started, was like a drug I couldn't get enough of. When it was denied me I became as frantic as an addict deprived of a fix. Once, when I was late for a rendezvous, I ripped my wallet in two in a frenzy to pay the cab driver. She had held back for months. She had let me nap beside her but not sleep with her. I had seen her body but was not allowed to touch it. Her kisses had moved tantalizingly from my cheek to the corner of my mouth, but no further. She had deliberately let passion grow before letting it loose in a flood. Being older, she possessed an inner discipline and power over her emotions that were unknown to me. She knew from experience that this pent-up passion, once released, produced gratification a thousand times more sublime than had we succumbed to it from the beginning.

To Mohamed's surprise, I started taking the car out by myself. In anticipation of a late-night rendezvous, I'd leave it two blocks away where it wouldn't be seen by Señor Bermudez, who sometimes cruised the street jealously checking to see if there were any cars parked outside her house. The upstairs floor which she occupied had nine windows: three in the living room, two in the kitchen, one in the bath, and three in the bedroom. When she was out, she always left the bathroom light on. Standing beneath a palm tree and listening to the sounds of the Moroccan night, I gazed at that single illuminated window, my beacon of love. Dogs barked, frogs groaned, and the muezzin called the faithful to evening prayer. From somewhere came the sound of drumming. During the summer there are weddings every night in Tangier. Processions of beribboned cars race by with horns honking. The whole city, it seems, was celebrating the rituals of marriage, but I don't think anyone was more excited by the prospect of impending love than me.

We had a secret arrangement. If she returned home alone, she would turn on the kitchen and bedroom lights, thus illuminating six windows. This was the signal for me to come up. But, if she had company, she turned on the living room light as well, illuminating all nine windows, which meant that my term of waiting was extended and became aggravated by a ferocious sexual impatience.

When the living room light went out again, meaning that her guest had departed, I leaped from beneath my palm tree and entered the house by a side door. Prostrate on a pile of sheepskins, the nightwatchman was used to seeing me bound by like a sprinter out of his blocks. Taking the steps four at a time, I raced upstairs and tapped on her door. Already in her nightgown, she opened to receive me.

✳

Africa did not tell me about her former lovers until we became lovers. Every Sunday after church, she said, Señor Bermudez used to send the official car to bring her to the Residencia, a colonnaded mansion set at the end of a long drive lined with palms. It was there, after a leisurely Spanish lunch, that she and the Consul used to make love during the hour of the siesta.

She insisted she wasn't his mistress any longer, just a friend of the family. Señor Bermudez consulted her when he had problems with his wife, and he still sent the consular car, a shiny black Mercedes, when she returned from trips to Madrid. She continued to go to the Residencia, but only for lunch. Instead of making love during the afternoon siesta, Don Carlos napped alone while she sipped tea and made small talk with Señora Bermudez.

Africa had spent her twenties in Madrid, working for UNESCO. I developed a nostalgia for those years. I wanted to know everything about them. She described them, with a note of resignation.

'You have an interesting job, a cozy place to live, and a few good friends you see regularly. You go out to dinner once a week, and take a trip once a year. Nothing ever really happens, but one is comfortable and, before you know it, ten years have gone by.'

There is about Africa an aura of sadness, an ineffable longing that comes, perhaps, from having lived so many years alone. This yearning for the unattainable overflowed onto the physical side, manifesting itself in a kind of sensual explicitness and almost manic obsession with how things taste, smell and feel. The seaweed-covered rocks we walked on, she said, were like 'soft wet rugs' beneath her feet. The baby eels she loved to eat felt like 'live tagliatelle' swimming inside her mouth.

The legacy of those years surfaced, from time to time, in the form of gentlemen callers from Madrid. The French violinist, the South American novelist, and the Hungarian *émigré* publisher – they all turned up in Tangier. To keep me from feeling jealous, Africa assured me that these visitors belonged to her past. She made them stay in a hotel, but the appearance of these older men made me understand that her loving ways in bed were the result of having had experienced teachers. Like Señor Bermudez, these sophisticated Europeans remembered, and they could not forget, what a passionate, attentive lover she was.

Then slowly, almost without my noticing it, she began to withdraw. Her social life became more hectic, and I saw less of her, because she was preparing herself for a flight from home. Right up until the eve of her departure, everybody wanted more of her time. The idea for a new book had suddenly blossomed inside the head of the lady novelist, and it needed transcribing. Fearful of being left alone, the widow on the Mountain grew more demanding. Africa obliged by doing the cooking and shopping and spending more nights there.

✳

Africa's in South America now. The long-awaited letter from UNESCO finally arrived, confirming an important administrative post in Cuzco, with a mission to distribute books and reorganize the rural school system that had been disrupted by the revolution.

I begged her not to go, but no amount of pleading could detain her. She moved her uncle Moyses and his wife into the house to look after her brothers. Like a bird that must respond to a migratory urge, she left in the middle of the night without saying goodbye.

A white envelope lay on my desk at the American Library. It looked like a death sentence. I recognized the handwriting — a childish scrawl that seemed to epitomize everything that was bent and broken within her. I stared at it for a few minutes before opening it.

If I were able to love you, Norman, and you loved me — then how I would love you!

'But I do love you!' I shouted into my classroom. The students tittered.

I could almost see her smiling. 'And I'll always love you. Wherever I am.'

'Do you think you'll ever get married?' I once asked her.

She had thought about it for a minute. 'Maybe when I'm sixty. For companionship.'

Her Peruvian friend will be waiting for her, I suppose. They'll scale the Andes and get that restaurant above the snowline going.

On my way to the American Library I sometimes

stop the car outside her house and look up at that row of windows where she gave me so much pleasure. And my path takes me past the gate of the Spanish Consulate. The Moroccan policeman in his sentry box eyes me suspiciously while I gaze down the row of manicured palms. Perhaps he suspects that Harry's old briefcase which now I carry contains a bomb, but I just can't help lingering a few more minutes. Curiosity and a kind of poignant jealousy keep my eyes fixed on the villa where Africa and the Consul, after a leisurely Spanish lunch, used to make love during the hour of the siesta.

✳

For several weeks I puttered around the house, went for walks in the garden, and gazed at my reflection in the fish pond. It looked all wobbly. I lay in the hammock wondering what I was going to do next. Fatima and Mohamed watched and waited; they were asking themselves the same thing.

With the onset of autumn, the wet wind began to blow, and the Old Mountain dripped with moisture. Predictably, my asthma started acting up again. The nights grew longer as breathing became a chore. The doctor renewed his visits, but I knew in advance what his advice would be. Pulling up stakes was the last thing I wanted to do, but he had already convinced me that in Tangier I would never be cured.

The expenses of the funeral, although not great by American standards, had further depleted my funds to the point where I could no longer afford to pay rent on the house. I informed the real estate agent that I was giving it up and, as Alice had foreseen, I sold the car.

The last days were gloomy ones. Fatima and Mohamed could not hide their dejection. I filled two big Moroccan baskets with Alice's clothes and left them on the doorstep of the convent in the middle of the night. I didn't want to have to explain where I had got them.

Fatima promised she would take care of my books, and I left Harry's watch with Mohamed for safe keeping.

'Now you know I'll be back,' I said.

Boarding the night train for Marrakesh, I took my place among strangers. The feeling of melancholy induced by riding on a train at night revived childhood memories of lying in a hospital ward, also at night. I was alone among people I did not know, confined to a space I could not leave. My fate was in the hands of others. There is a helplessness or passivity in both situations.

During the night the compartment filled with soldiers. It was cold, and one of them spread his cape over me. After that I slept better.

When I woke up the soldiers had gone, the sun was shining, and the train was standing in a little railroad station somewhere in southern Morocco. The station walls had been painted pink, and the flower boxes were crowded with red geraniums. The stationmaster, in his pyjamas and official blue cap, was standing by the train chatting with the conductor.

When the train began to move, the windows sprouted arms of passengers waving goodbye. The stationmaster walked beside the train to the end of the platform, touched two fingers to the visor on his cap, and saluted. I waved and he waved back. Little did he know that one day I hoped to find a situation like his: a place of my own to look after, surrounded by people who know me, and comforted by the reasonable assurance that things would stay the same.

We headed out across the empty plain. Long rides across arid lands never tire me; space, in the end, always leaves me refreshed. From the train I was viewing the distant flocks of sheep and modest dwellings barely distinguishable from the earth. The tiny figures of men were almost invisible beneath the wide, luminous sky.

On one of our rides through the countryside outside Tangier Harry had remarked that the people like the ones who inhabit the African plains are in the majority; but in all the congresses of the world they are denounced as being resistant to change and mainly concerned with survival.

And what's wrong with that? I wanted to know.

Unlike ourselves, he said, who can't even cook, they are self-sufficient. They know how to till the soil and make their own bread. They are both shepherds and experts at the fine art of weaving. They fashion their homes from the earth. For them, oil comes from the olive. Labouring beneath the sky, they feel close to God.

✳

At the Marrakesh railroad station there was a terrific bustle as the passengers tried to squeeze through a narrow gate. In Morocco they make you give your ticket back. I've never known what they do with them.

From the mob of excited people an arm was raised and waving. It was Moktar's. He warmly shook my hand as though the good old days had returned. I didn't have the heart to say they hadn't. He led the way to the carriage. The sun was shining, the birds were singing, and the perfume from orange blossoms filled the air.

All about the carriage, people were hugging and laughing. Fathers in uniform were holding up children to see how much they'd grown. Some mothers looked on proudly while others, who should have resolved to save their complaints until they got their men into the house, just couldn't hold back and were letting it all go in a torrent. Shy lovers were holding hands and looking at each other's feet. Despite that old feeling of envy, it made me feel good to watch them.

At the hotel they gave me my old room back. I just didn't have the energy to unpack. I lay on the bed, with my hands behind my head, and stared at the ceiling. At three o'clock in the afternoon the hot desert wind began to blow. I was troubled by a low moan through the shutters that seemed to contain a comfortless message intended for myself.

✳

At five o'clock in the morning roosters were crowing all over the city. The bus station was located just a block from the hotel. At all hours of the day and night buses leave Marrakesh for Saharan destinations whose names are hard to pronounce. I'd located some of these places on my map. The desert looked so big that I hardly knew where to enter it, let alone what to do when I got there, except to breathe the dry air. Dotted lines look like roads of some sort, or camel tracks, or maybe they are just dry riverbeds. Most just peter out in the middle of nowhere.

Neither did the tourist bureau give out much information. Although the countryside around the Marrakesh oasis is dry and desert-like, you have to cross the Atlas Mountains, as Alice and I had done, to reach the desert proper. I'd heard some frightening stories about the Sahara. For example, the temperature can change as much as a hundred degrees in a single day, causing rocks to explode with a sound like gunfire. Sandstorms rasping over the rough surface of the desert generate enough static electricity to make your hair stand up on the top of your head. And on days when there's not a cloud in the sky, a dry gorge can suddenly fill with a rampaging torrent of water that destroys everything in its path.

Moreover, the silence of the desert can be so profound that when you stand perfectly still the only sound you can hear is the beating of your heart. If you can stick it out, however, you eventually grow accustomed to the mineral landscape which has inspired so many prophets. Not only that, you can get to like the desert so much that you don't want to leave for any reason, and have to be dragged out, sometimes raving. The Moroccans have a saying about the desert: *When God made the world, He gave His head to the peoples of the north; He gave His heart to the peoples of the south; but when it came to the desert, He didn't have anything left, so He gave it His soul.*

One point everyone agrees on is that in the desert the relative humidity is low, the pollen count is next to zero, and mould is non-existent. Anybody, whether he suffers from a respiratory ailment or not, breathes easier and is bound to feel invigorated.

The day had already begun, but stars ranged across a sky that was not quite black. The circle of light and activity that surrounded the bus seemed strangely undersized, as though I were viewing it from a great height. Even in the middle of a big city like Marrakesh, a hush prevails. Maybe it's the silence from the sky that diminishes men and prompts them to keep their voices down.

The bus was being loaded and readied. A lot of people were moving around in the dark. There is no day or night for Moroccans; they don't divide up the hours like we do. Cupping a glass of coffee in my hands, I sleepily sized up the bus and took note of its special characteristics. This one was pale green and had a pink stripe running down the middle.

The motor roared. 'Where's the Nazarene?' the driver asked. He laughed when he realized that I was standing right beside him. The mechanic found me a seat up front where 'seeing is better.' Patting my new blanket, he placed the suitcase in the rack above.

The trip over the Atlas Mountains was cold and dangerous. Wrapped in my blanket, however, I felt warm. Moreover, I was surrounded by passengers with whom, for the next few hours at least, I would share an identical fate. The chanting to Allah went on and on. I like these songs of Africa. You don't have to understand the words to recognize the message of mingling pain and joy. Everybody in Morocco knows these songs by heart, and I couldn't resist humming along with them. After a while I dozed off, and there was no tension before sleep.

Opening my eyes, I looked out upon grey snow-fields overhung by veils of mist. A dog was searching for scraps, and men were shovelling. We crossed the pass and came out on the other side of the mountains beneath blue skies. The clouds had sunk to the valley floor, making islands of the peaks.

The bus stopped for a man to board. His village had come out to see him off. A group of young women in white woollen djellabas and colourful headdresses was singing. A small boy was weeping. His eyes were red. He had to be restrained from running after the bus.

A large black woman occupied the seat next to mine. She was swathed from head to foot in a silvery indigo robe that exuded a sweet dusty odour. She had led the chanting in a passionate, husky voice. I gathered she was an entertainer of some sort.

'Don't you have a gentleman or lady with you?' she asked.

I said no.

'It's better that way,' she said, patting my hand and smiling. 'Quieter.'

The man sitting behind us was talking to a sheep on the floor. Another father had wrapped his son in his burnoose. He held the boy in his arms, rocking him gently until he fell asleep.

We arrived in Ouarzazate at noon. As the motor was making a loud noise, the driver announced there would be a delay. I took a walk through the town. A heavy cold wind was blowing down from the mountains, and groups of young men were standing around with their hands in their pockets. There was nothing for them to do. With some time to kill I thought this would be a good opportunity to take Miss Toledano's advice and visit the hammam.

An old man in a loincloth welcomed me inside. He handed me a clean towel and showed me a changing room where I could leave my clothes. I had no idea how much to take off: did a Christian enter a Muslim hammam completely naked? Rather than take a chance of offending someone, I kept my underwear on.

There being no lockers or hooks to hang things on, I made a tidy bundle on the floor, next to some others. My last travellers checks and my passport were in there. I didn't know where else to leave them. The hammam is like the house of God, the old man assured me, nodding with approval at my boxer shorts. Everything is safe here. But when I showed him my passport, he picked up my bundle, stuffed it into a cupboard, locked it, and handed me the key.

A thick door opened into the baths. Water was running everywhere, and waxy bodies were writhing in the gloom. We passed through the warm room where fathers patiently scrubbed their sons; some sleepy fellows were sprawled on their backs by the wall, snoring peacefully.

The next room was hotter and rang with the cries of young men showing off. They swung from bars and did push-ups on the floor. Amidst shouts for water and the general hilarity, empty buckets rolled about, and streams of soapsuds slid toward the drains.

Another heavy door closed behind us. Bathed in the dim light of a distant bulb, the marble floor of the very hot room reflected an oily gleam. My guide, a professional washer whose body after years in the baths had developed the supple shine and smoothness of an eel, flooded the floor with water and made me stretch out on my stomach. His feet trod my back, forcing me to release all my air. After massaging my hands and feet, he lay me across his knees and cracked my spine.

Following these exercises, he doused me with water and rubbed me all over with a disk of palm wood. The massage combined with the heat to open my pores. The eel-man grinned at the appearance of the hidden dirt, which he flushed away with buckets of warm water.

Shampoo followed soap, and I was taken to the center of the room and made to squat. Bucket after bucket was sloshed over me. Lines of buckets filled from the smoking spigot were slid across the floor. Hot water became warm, turned cool, and was suddenly ice-cold. I was gasping for breath.

He led the way along a damp corridor to a private room. I lay down on a straw mat, towels were wrapped around me, and sections of orange were offered. Africa was right: the languid after-effect of the bath, the soft towels, the taste of fresh orange in my mouth, and above all the sense of being wonderfully clean produced a feeling of relaxation and peace. I shut my eyes and slept for a few minutes.

✳

The bus was finally repaired. We hadn't covered more than a few miles when we stopped again. The sun was going down. Everybody got out, and the bus was surrounded by the woolly forms of people praying. I walked off into the desert to touch a telephone pole for good luck. All that could be heard was the sound of the wind sweeping the rocks and singing through the wires. A donkey stood by itself in the distance. Its head was down. I returned to the bus whistling 'Onward Christian Soldiers.'

We were supposed to go straight through to Zagora, but the driver was tired, and we stopped in one of those desert villages whose names I can never say right. Agdz, it is spelled. The passengers jumped out and disappeared into the dark. Everyone, it seemed, had some place to go to. I looked for a place to sleep and was shown a bed in a café. Two sheets and an army blanket for five dirhams, or about a dollar. I was prepared to take it if given another blanket. They refused and turned their backs. They didn't care where I slept. I crossed the square to another café, a clean one. Two men from the bus were preparing to sleep. One had rented a cot, another a mat. The owner had his own mat with blankets. They looked at me standing in the doorway and pointed to where they would sleep.

'*Et moi?*' I asked.

This brought uproarious laughter, and they prepared a pad for me. A mat, two blankets, and two clean sheets for four dirhams. I slept in what was once the dining-room. I could hear them laughing in the next room. '*Et moi?*' they kept repeating with laughter, even after the lamp had been blown out.

Before dawn we made another departure. 'Where's the Nazarene?' the driver asked the mechanic. They pretended they couldn't see me. I didn't mind being different; furthermore I was willing to receive their protection.

Down the Dra Valley in darkness we went. The lights conked out at six am, but we continued. A pale sun, almost Nordic, appeared. Dawn revealed the silhouettes of mud castles floating in the mist. A tremendous volume of water flowing in the river. I wondered if I should be exploring the desert by canoe.

We arrived in Zagora at seven. I walked down the street and stood before the camel sign. The last time

I'd seen it, Alice had been with me. The sign had made me imagine a desert trip, but she had talked of death. Each had thought the other was joking, but what we said had turned out to be true. She was dead, and I was in this place.

While I was standing there a Jeep pulled up. Some German tourists jumped out and began to snap photos.

In the afternoon we set off once more. With the desert all around, a new kind of trip was beginning. Everyone on the bus was dressed in the indigo blue robes of the Sahara.

At a place called Tagonite three girls got on. The backs of their hands were elaborately tattooed with patterns as dark as the blue of their robes. I sat behind two of the girls. The other girl sat in front of them. When she turned to talk to her friends, I was astonished. Her body was completely enveloped in blue cloth. Only the hands and feet showed. I was reminded of a puppet show, or a play with masks.

Tagonite. The signpost:

Foum	160
Oued Driss	
M'Hamid	27
Hassi Beida	60
Tabelbala	350
Tindouf	360
Tintouchai	135
Timbuktoo	50 days

✳

174

Suddenly, the sand. Dunes floated in the distance, above a mercury lake of mirage. Trailing a cloud of dust, we charged through the arch of M'Hamid. This was the end of the line. The road went no further. From M'Hamid, the bus driver informed me, one must proceed on camel or by truck. As usual everyone got out and disappeared. They all had something to do. The sun was going down, and smoke from cookfires was rising from villages hidden behind palm trees. This was the Dra River valley, but there was no water in it. The sand had swallowed the flood. My canoe trip would have been a fiasco.

Picking up my suitcase, I carried it out into the desert and set it down on a sand dune. The dunes of M'Hamid are not high, but they are desert dunes that creep with the wind. I noticed a weird sound – a ringing. Or was it the silence? There was no telling. Part of the mystery and another thing to find out about. I stayed on the dune and watched the same group of German tourists arrive in their Jeep. They wanted to see the sand, take pictures, and return to the hotel in Zagora where there was a bar and a swimming pool. I didn't blame them; Alice and I had done the same thing.

A few hundred yards off the sand ended, and a flat red plain stretched away toward some low hills in the distance. Out on the plain stood a *koubba*, or another saint's tomb, that dot the landscape of Morocco. Illuminated by the sun's departing rays, its white-washed dome glowed like a pearl against the swarthy background of the desert. Unlike the one I had visited in the Atlas Mountains, it didn't look as though anyone lived there. A crack in the dome needed mending, and part of the surrounding wall had fallen down. The whole place could use a fresh coat of paint. I resolved to make it my final destination for the day.

I realize that my life out here is going to be different from the life of almost everyone else in the world. Certainly it will be nothing like it was before. Yet it seems so natural to be here that, already, I can hardly believe that I lived anywhere else, or that I once had a life like anyone else.

But if I want to recount this story of how I came to be here, I'll have to get it straight in my own head first. One way to do that is to write it out. Because one thing did not lead to another, or at least in any way that I can see. Yet when I look back on my former life, strange as it now appears, I cannot conceive of how it could have led me anywhere but here.

Picking up my suitcase again, I walked toward the *koubba*. The sun was resting on the horizon, and my shadow stretched towards infinity. My shoes crunched on the gravel. That was the only sound, it seemed, in all creation.

ALSO AVAILABLE BY JOHN HOPKINS

The Tangier Diaries

John Hopkins

'Every page drips with memories' – William S. Burroughs

'July 14 – La Place de la Kasbah: We parked the motorcycle by a high white wall with pink geraniums spilling down . . . We entered a courtyard paved with green and red tiles. White Moorish arches ran along one side. A gnarled old fig tree, whose branches were so heavy they had to be supported by chains – the chains themselves had long ago become embedded in the wood – shaded the patio with its broad leafy expanse. This was a tree, our host explained, where Samuel Pepys wrote his Tangier diaries back in 1683, when England ruled this city. Green figs as big as your fist hung precariously over our heads. A bust of Seneca scowled from the top of a Roman column. Water splashed in a little fountain. A yellow-crusted cockatoo hung upside down in a cage, shrieking, 'Patatas fritas, Patatas fritas!' . . . The scene was Mediterranean and timeless. It could have been a house in Ancient Rome or Greece, Leptis Magna or Alexandria.'

'Hopkins writes as powerfully of places as of people, capturing the steamy bustle of the Kasbah market and the awesome mystery of the Sahara'
– Michael Arditti, *Daily Mail*

'He draws the reader into the daily life of what he describes as the "Saigon of the Sahara", with tales of his encounters with the likes of William Burroughs, Malcolm Forbes, Wilfred Thesiger, Timothy Leary and Rudolf Nureyev . . . a chronicle of an era that has disappeared forever' – *Independent on Sunday*

'The Sixties are vividly described by a young American who surged out of Princeton with a friend to Peru, Europe and eventually on to Tangier. Hopkins records his apprenticeship as a novelist and conveys "the sheer glory and joy of being alive in this town". A hit' – Judy Cooke, *Mail on Sunday*

'These fascinating pages are crammed with reminiscences of the glitterazia who once made up Tangier society. Gossip, intrigue, or the extremes of native wealth and poverty are recorded with unerring skill'
– Richard Edmonds, *Birmingham Post*

'A fascinating glimpse of the unique time and place in modern literary history. Hopkins offers an extended insider's perspective on a milieu presided over by the enigmatic Paul Bowles and his wife, the gifted writer Jane Bowles'
– *San Francisco Sunday Examiner & Chronicle*

'Paul Theroux without the pretence and arrogance . . . crafted by a sensitive and generous intelligence' – *Arkansas Democrat Gazette*

ALSO AVAILABLE BY JOHN HOPKINS

The South American Diaries

John Hopkins

Following the success of his Tangier Diaries, John Hopkins turns his eye to a youth spent travelling around South America. After graduating from Princeton University, Hopkins went to Peru with the intention of buying a coffee plantation. He travelled widely in the Andes and the jungle and floated down the Amazon on a balsa raft. He also took part in a number of archaeological digs, collecting pre-Colombian artefacts from the desert valleys.

Hopkins returned to Peru in 1964; 1970 saw him travelling by dugout canoe through the jungle rivers of Guatemala visiting remote Mayan cities. He went up the Amazon from Belém to Manaus to Iquitos and meandered through Peru and Bolivia spending several months on a cattle ranch in Paraguay. Hopkins rounds off his marathon travels with visits to Argentina and Uruguay, ending up in Bahia in north-east Brazil.

Doubtful Partners
John Haylock

The latest novel from the author of *Eastern Exchange* is a light-hearted look at the barriers and frustrations in close attachments – especially those doubtful partnerships in which communication is entirely physical.

'If there is one thing to bring out the candid in Haylock, it is the ins and outs of intimate intercourse' – *The Times*

Eastern Exchange
John Haylock

'For those with a fascination for eccentric lives, Haylock's book is a little gem, the record of an extraordinarily interesting life' – Ian Buruma, *Sunday Telegraph*

Eddy: The Life of Edward Sackville-West
Michael De-la-Noy

Heir to Knole and a peerage, novelist, discerning critic and brilliant pianist, the intimate of Bloomsbury writers and painters, Edward Sackville-West was born with the proverbial silver spoon in his mouth. Through diaries and previously unpublished letters, we see a life dogged a chronic ill-health and a masochistic psychological make-up.

'Nobody can fail to respect the skill and industry which De-la-Noy has devoted to bringing Eddy Sackville-West back to life in this elegant and sympathetic biography' – *Sunday Times*

His Mistress's Voice
Gillian Freeman

Victorian London: Simon, a young Jewish widower with a small son emigrates from Warsaw to London's East End, staying with family there until he takes up the position of cantor at a smart Reform synagogue off Lower Regent Street. His liaison with Phoebe Fenelle, a leading actress of the day leads to dire consequences for her husband – or does it?

'Her writing is pure pleasure' – *Evening Standard*

When Memory Dies
A. Sivanandan

A three-generational saga of a Sri Lankan family's search for coherence and continuity in a country broken by colonial occupation and riven by ethnic wars. Winner of the Sagittarius Prize and shortlisted for the Commonwealth Writers Prize. FOURTH IMPRESSION.

'Haunting ... with an immense tenderness. The extraordinary poetic tact of this book makes it unforgettable' – John Berger, *Guardian*

The Last Kabbalist of Lisbon
Richard Zimler

A literary mystery set among secret Jews living in Lisbon in 1506 when, during Passover celebrations, some two thousand Jewish inhabitants were murdered in a pogrom. THE INTERNATIONAL BESTSELLER. TENTH IMPRESSION.

'Remarkable erudition and compelling imagination, an American Umberto Eco' – Francis King, *Spectator*

Night Letters
Robert Dessaix

Every night for twenty nights in a hotel room in Venice, a man recently diagnosed with HIV writes a letter home to a friend. He describes not only the kaleidoscopic journey he has just made from Switzerland across northern Italy to Venice, but reflects on questions of mortality, seduction and the search for paradise.

'Dessaix writes with great elegance, with passion, compassion, and sly wit. Literally a wonderful book' – John Banville

Double Act
Fiona Pitt-Kethley

'This poetry collection reads like it's been written by a sexually charged Philip Larkin. Both witty and scathing, it avoids the tender eroticism often employed when discussing sex and instead goes straight for the jugular' – *D›tour Magazine*

Tomorrow
Elisabeth Russell Taylor

In August 1960, a number of ill-assorted guests gather at a small hotel on the Danish island of Møn. Among them is Elisabeth Danziger, whose happy memories of growing up in a brilliant and gifted family are overshadowed by darker ones, over which she struggles to achieve control.

'A memorable and poignant novel made all the more heartbreaking by the quiet dignity of its central character and the restraint of its telling' – Shena Mackay

Present Fears
Elisabeth Russell Taylor

'It is hard to pinpoint what makes these stories so unsettling. Their worlds – some border territory between genteel suburbia and dreamland – are imagined with an eerie thoroughness. The inhabitants are all out of kilter, and terrifyingly fragile; spinsterish middle-agers paralysed by sexual fear; anxious children in the centre of parental power games. Russell Taylor's abrupt, elegantly engineered anti-climaxes leave the reader with the disquieting feeling of waiting for the other shoe to fall' – Sam Leith, *Observer*. SECOND IMPRESSION.

Isabelle
John Berger and Nella Bielski

A compelling recreation of the life of Isabelle Eberhardt. SECOND IMPRESSION.

'A tantalizing enigma, Berger and Bielski's filmic approach is appropriate to her literally dramatic life, and the symmetry of the imagery is an indication of the artistry of this work' – *Observer*

Fear of Mirrors
Tariq Ali

Lovers want to know the truth, but they do not always want to tell it. For some East Germans, the fall of Communism was like the end of a long and painful love affair; free to tell the truth at last, they found they no longer wanted to hear it.

'When Ali's imagination goes wild he is superb' – *New Statesman*